Rowan's mind was ⟨...⟩ the black shape and the scream
... whinny? It wa⟨...⟩ had been its shoes
on the road, skidd⟨...⟩

'I know! It's that pony Charlie was ⟨...⟩ w
it – loose on the down last week! They tried to c⟨...⟩ t
but couldn't. He said a few people had tried to catch it.
No-one knows where it's come from.'

'It's a disgrace! Animals roaming loose! We might have
been killed!'

The Swallow Tale is the first title in K.M. Peyton's
High Horse series about Rowan and her friends, the
Hawes family.

Also available by K.M. Peyton, and published
by Corgi books:

THE SWALLOW SUMMER
SWALLOW, THE STAR

THE WILD BOY AND QUEEN MOON
THE BOY WHO WASN'T THERE

For younger readers

POOR BADGER

For beginner readers

WINDY WEBLEY

K.M. PEYTON

THE SWALLOW TALE

Illustrated by the author

CORGI BOOKS

THE SWALLOW TALE

A CORGI BOOK : 0 552 52807 2

First publication in Great Britain by Doubleday,
a division of Transworld Publishers Ltd

PRINTING HISTORY
Doubleday edition published 1995
Corgi edition published 1996
Reissued 1998

Young Corgi Books are published by Transworld Publishers Ltd,
61–63 Uxbridge Road, London W5 5SA,
in Australia by Transworld Publishers (Australia) Pty Ltd,
15–25 Helles Avenue, Moorebank, NSW 2170,
and in New Zealand by Transworld Publishers (NZ) Ltd,
3 William Pickering Drive, Albany, Auckland.

Typeset in Monotype Bembo by
Phoenix Typesetting, Ilkley, West Yorkshire

Printed and bound in Great Britain by
Cox & Wyman Ltd, Reading, Berkshire.

To Primrose

CHAPTER ONE

Rowan was silent, sitting in the car beside her father as they came over the brow of the hill above Long Bottom. Her father was in a bad mood, she could tell. He usually was when he came home, after the hassle of commuting from London. He wasn't a country man at all and Rowan suspected that he was regretting their move out of suburbia and into the country. Last year she had dreaded leaving London, but now she would dread moving back even more.

He drove too fast, fresh off the motorway. It was going dusk. The hedges were high and the early sloe blossom made a blurred wall, shutting out the view.

'Whatever—?'

The brakes screamed. Rowan was flung violently forward into her seat-belt as the car skidded sideways and slammed up against the left-hand bank. Soft earth rained on the windows and sparks spun across the road ahead. Sparks? Rowan could not think, shocked rigid. A black shape like a flying witch's cloak filled the windscreen and then disappeared into the sloe hedge. There was a crashing sound and what sounded like an animal scream mixed with the awful noise of John Watkins swearing. His new Mondeo was his most darling possession.

He leapt out of the car to see the damage and Rowan followed warily. There was glass over the road, plain and coloured.

'My headlight! And the indicator! God in heaven – just what I need! Look at it!'

Rowan looked. On the bent metal frame of the headlight blood and fur were imbedded.

'It was an animal! Look! You've injured it!'

'Injured it? Pity I didn't break its ruddy neck!'

'You can't leave it. It might have a broken leg!'

Rowan ran to the hedge, standing on tiptoe to peer over. She was small for her eleven years and had difficulty making anything out. The black animal had blended into the dusk. It had gone through the hedge – she could see the broken twigs – and into the grass field, but the field was large, stretching right down to the back gardens of the village houses below and she could see nothing moving.

She helped her father kick the glass into the ditch. The front light still worked but shone crookedly sideways.

'That's a garage job! But I can claim insurance – animals are the owner's responsibility—'

'We can't just leave it,' Rowan said. 'You hit it. It's hurt.'

'Serve it right – bally animal—'

Rowan thought her father was ridiculous. Her mind was full of the black shape and the scream . . . whinny? It was a pony! The sparks had been its shoes on the road, skidding. A pony—

'I know! It's that pony Charlie was talking about! He saw it – loose on the down last week! They tried to catch it but couldn't. He said a few people had tried to catch it. No-one knows where it's come from.'

'It's a disgrace! Animals roaming loose! We might have been killed!'

Sometimes her father was very childish. It wouldn't be wise to tell him he had been going too fast. Best to wait until he cooled down.

No way could they leave that pony injured, but he didn't seem to realize that. They drove down through the village to their house, called Home Farm, in the middle. What had once been the farm's barns had been converted into smart houses behind it. The burglar lights came on as the car swung into the drive.

Rowan waited until her father had huffed and puffed about the accident to his wife, and then stated that it was their duty to follow up the wounded animal.

'If you think I'm going to go out chasing the damned thing in the dark—'

'Charlie will catch it. Just run me up to the farm and I'll tell them what's happened – or I'll go on my bike – we'll do it—'

'It's dark. Daddy will run you, won't you, darling? I do think Rowan's right, dear. But won't you have your tea first?'

'No. It's urgent. I can go on my bike, Dad, honest.'

'Don't be silly,' he said.

Why did parents think there were murderers lurking all over the place? Rowan liked the village darkness with just the house windows showing golden lamps and flickering television, but her father was already agitating for street lighting. When they had had their accident he had been driving her home from her piano lesson, which she could easily have gone to on her bike (save it was a bit hilly).

'Come on, then. Jump in.'

With one headlamp doused, he drove her up the hill. The farm where Charlie lived, High Hawes, was half a mile up on the right, a scrambling old farm whose barns had been turned not into houses but into stables. John Watkins was impressed by the fact that the family that lived there was called Hawes as well as the house, but this was actually a coincidence, not a sign of ancient family bloodlines. Certainly the family had lived there for many years – they didn't count as 'incomers' like the Watkins – but they were not real farmers like Mr Flint and Mr Bailey down in the valley – they hadn't enough land for that, only fifty acres. Mr Hawes was said to live on his wits, although he called himself a horse dealer. He had five children who were all into horses, and an absent-minded wife called Joan who was a brilliant cook.

Mr Watkins pulled up in the entrance to the yard and let Rowan out.

'Don't be all night, now. Ring me if you want a lift back.'

'No. I'll be all right.' Did he think she had no legs?

To her relief he backed out and drove away. Rowan walked up the slope into the main yard where the lights were shining. There were loose-boxes all round and eager heads looked over doors at the sounds coming from the feed shed. Rowan had discovered her own paradise on earth here since coming to Long Bottom and haunted this place, doing lowly chores to earn her acceptance.

'Charlie?'

She went towards the feed shed and Charlie came out, hearing the car drive away. Charlie was seventeen, the second eldest of the children after his sister Josephine. Josephine never spoke to Rowan, but Charlie was easy-going and friendly.

'What's up?'

Rowan told him.

'Several people have seen that pony,' he said. 'I've seen it up on the downs above us. But no-one can catch it. It's been down by our fences several times but every time you go near it it runs off.'

'It's in Mr Bailey's big cow field now.'

'It jumps like a stag. If we go after it, it'll jump out.'

'But it's hurt. We gave it a real crack, bashed in the headlight.'

'Fair enough. I'll come down with you. We can't leave it if it's injured. I'll just finish feeding and we'll go down in the Land-Rover.'

Charlie was tall and gangly, long-legged. He looked fantastic on a horse. The Hawes children all rode brilliantly, from cool Josephine down to Shrimp the nine-year-old. Rowan had first met them – the younger ones – on the school bus. She got on well with the two middle ones, Lizzie and Hugh, (she had been put in the same class as Hugh) but Charlie was her darling. He had a gypsyish look, with thick black curls, very dark eyes and spare, hollow cheeks. The others were all fair or mousy and quite ordinary in looks. Rowan was slightly nervous of Charlie, liking him so much. She would never have presumed to ask him favours ordinarily, but an injured pony – one was bound to seek help.

He told his parents where he was going – Hugh and Shrimp wanted to come too but were not allowed – and Rowan scrambled into the Land-Rover beside him. She was so excited she could feel her heart bumping. If they caught the pony . . . no-one knew who it belonged to . . . finders keepers? Would her father agree? She longed to have her own pony.

'It's not a scruff,' Charlie said. 'It's nice – a Welshman by the look of him.'

They drove down the hill and turned right when they came to the village street. Rowan had a glimpse through the windows of her father getting himself a gin and tonic from the sideboard, to calm his nerves. He would be in a dreadful temper over the car. The Hawes parents didn't fuss at all and never drank gin and tonic. Rowan sighed. Life as lived by the Hawes had been a revelation to her. They all worked incredibly hard, and yet there was no coercion. The ponies and horses were a full-time job and they enjoyed it and accepted it, on top of working hard at school. The three of them at school were bright, and never took days off, in spite of all they had to do at home.

They drove up the street to the Baileys' farm, which was the last building. It was called Low Bottom. There was a house further up called, amazingly, High Bottom, and just below it one called Middle Bottom, and in the village

14

street there was a Bottoms Up, which Rowan thought was great but her parents thought vulgar.

'I'll just call and tell Ted Bailey what we're up to. Don't want him to think he's got rustlers in the field.'

They got out of the Land-Rover and Rowan walked on past the stockyards to where the gate let into the field. It was going dark and a mist lay across the bottom of the hill, out of which Ted Bailey's Friesian cows loomed menacingly. Their breath made clouds around their monotonously revolving jaws and their sad eyes stared at her. Rowan, a London girl, wasn't sure about cows.

'What you doin'?'

Rowan jumped. She turned and saw the farmer's daughter behind her, a square girl called Barbara. The Hawes called her Babar the Elephant, which she didn't seem to mind.

'There's a pony—' Rowan explained what had happened.

'Aar, I saw 'um. 'E's there.'

Babar talked like a simpleton, but got 100 per cent in maths. She had a straight no-nonsense fringe, very direct currant-bun eyes in a puddingy face, and always wore a brown

15

anorak and gumboots. She had a pony which she adored; it was a very odd shape – 'a Fell pony gone wrong, frightened by a thoroughbred weed' – according to Fred Hawes. Its name was Black Diamond.

('Sounds like beer,' Hugh said. His pony was called Cascade.

'Like washing-up liquid,' said Shrimp. Hugh threw his dirty sponge at her and she hit him with a sweat-scraper. They fought a lot, the Hawes.)

'I think he's hurt. He ran across in front of our car and we hit him.'

'We'll need to catch 'um then.'

Charlie came back, carrying a head-collar, and said, 'You got a few nuts in a bucket, Babar, that we can rattle at him?'

Babar plodded off in her gumboots and fetched the bait and they opened the gate and went in amongst the cows. It was all right with the others, Rowan found; she was terrified of being a fool in front of these calm country people. But she could still feel her heart lurching with excitement.

A black pony was hard to see in the mist-heavy dusk, but it gave itself away by a nervous snort up the hillside. They moved towards

16

the snort, but Charlie told the girls to hang back and went on with the bucket, talking softly into the mist. Shortly the pony came whirling down towards the gate, swerving past Charlie and skittering to a stop when he saw the girls. Rowan had a dazzled look at him, the head held high and wild, forelock on end, eyes shining, before he did an about-turn and went to join the cows.

'Oh, he's gorgeous!'

Babar said, 'Darned contrary. He'll never be caught, that one.'

Charlie came back. 'He's dead lame. He needs looking at.' Rowan had never noticed. 'We'll block off the drive out to the road, open the gate, drive off the cows and see if we can tempt him into the stockyard. Tie your pony up out in the yard, Babar, and that might attract him.'

He went and manoeuvred his Land-Rover so that it was athwart the drive, blocking off the road, and Babar fetched her pony from its stable and tied it up outside. Rowan saw why the Hawes tribe derided it, for it was a strange-looking beast, like an old-fashioned cab-horse, with large knees, a slightly swayed back, a hogged mane and a sad expression. It was a clipped-out black, a dull mousey colour, and looked as if it would have very hairy heels were they not clipped. Its tail looked as if the cows had been nibbling it.

'Darling Diamond,' Babar said, kissing it on the nose. Rowan was touched. Babar came back and went off to chase the cows away from the gate and Charlie told Rowan to stand just clear of the gate and try and deflect the pony in if it came her way.

'Wave your arms at it.'

Rowan was terrified she would mess up the whole operation, being so unsure of these large and unco-operative animals, but Charlie knew what he was doing and was able to catch the pony's attention with the rattling nuts in the bucket. Having attracted it, he walked slowly back towards the gate, shaking the bucket, and the pony followed hesitantly. Charlie walked into the stockyard and started feeding the nuts to Black Diamond, who made eager, starving noises as he dived his head into the bucket. This attracted the black pony and, as Rowan shrank back to make herself invisible, he walked through the gate and into the stockyard. Rowan nipped up and shut the gate into the field, and then the stockyard gate, and the pony was caught.

'Well done!' called Charlie.

He put the bucket down and managed to get the head-collar on without any difficulty. Black Diamond stood with tragic eyes, watching his feed disappearing down the other pony's throat.

'Great. Good work. That could have taken all night. We were lucky,' Charlie said.

'Clever,' said Babar, admiringly.

'It's nice. Worth the bother. Finders keepers, eh, Rowan?' Charlie winked at Rowan, and Rowan felt the heart-bumping excitement come back, suffocating her. If only—! To have this pony for her own . . . it was a wish that felt like madness. And as if in appeal, the pony lifted its head out of the empty bucket, looked straight at her and let out a deafening whinny.

The pony, even to her ignorant eyes, looked a beauty, as elegant and classy as Black Diamond was ill-bred. He was very dark brown or black, with a small snip of white between his nostrils and a star on his forehead. He stood about fourteen hands, and was strongly built, but with a fine neck and shoulder and a very pretty head.

'A Welshman,' Charlie said, 'With a dash of thoroughbred, I'd say.' He was looking at the pony's legs to find the damage. 'Hold him for me, will you?'

Rowan took the head-collar rope. She had never held a pony before. She could smell his hot, nervous breath on her hand and see the glint in his eye. He looked wild, but stood quietly, trembling.

There was a gash on his off foreleg just above the knee and the knee was swollen, but nothing terrible.

'He'll be stiff for a day or two. Have you got a stable for him down here, Babar? It wouldn't do him a lot of good to take him up to Hawes.'

'He can go next to Diamond, where my tack is. I'll clear it out.'

The stables were old, with worn hollows in the brick floors where once the cart-horses had stood, and long wooden mangers along the back wall. Babar moved her tack and Charlie threw in a couple of bales of straw to make a bed and Rowan led the pony behind Black Diamond into his new quarters. A wooden partition with iron railings separated the two. The wild pony seemed to want to stay with Diamond, which was what Charlie had reckoned on. Babar fetched him an armful of hay and a bucket of water, with which Charlie cleaned the injury, then Babar refilled it for the pony to drink. Charlie was so quick and practised that the whole operation only took a short time. He went off to tell Ted Bailey what had happened. Rowan waited for him, leaning over the stable door, unable to remove her eyes from this magic pony. It had leapt into her arms, she thought. It was hers by right.

''E's bin loose for a while,' Babar said. 'We seen 'um a few times. Will you keep 'um?'

'We'll have to tell the police.'

'They won't want to know,' Babar said. 'No-one's lookin' for 'um, not that we've 'eard.'

'How do you know? Are you sure?'

'No-one's bin round the market. That's where they come lookin'.'

'I would love to have him! But my father—' Her voice failed her. Her father was not an animal-lover. Especially of the animal that had damaged his beastly car. They had no field or stable, in spite of living in a house called Home Farm.

'You could keep 'um 'ere. Company for Diamond like.'

But Rowan knew she would prefer to keep him at High Hawes – should the luck ever come her way to own him.

Charlie came back and thanked Babar for her help. 'I'll come down and sort him out in the morning. Meanwhile he'll be safe shut away here. Good on yer, Babar.'

'Ta ra,' said Babar.

Charlie got back in the Land-Rover and Rowan climbed in beside him. She was boiling hot, still stirred up with excitement. The pony was magnificent!

'Do we have to tell the police?'

Charlie laughed. 'It's the drill, yes. You fancy him, then?'

'Oh yes!'

'He's very nice. Not a beginner's pony by the look of him, though.' Rowan knew she was a beginner but Charlie's condescension deflated her. Everybody could ride round here; even Babar the Elephant was an expert compared with herself. She was deluding herself, she knew, if she harboured dreams of owning that lovely pony.

'What we'll do,' Charlie said, as they drove

back into the village, ' – tomorrow morning I'll bring Hugh's camera down – it spits the films out straight away – you know the sort – and we'll take a couple of shots in to the police in town. I've got to go in anyway to Arnold's dump – I've got an old engine he wants. You can come with me if you like, and we'll find out if he's been reported missing.'

'Babar says he hasn't. Not on the market, at least.'

'They generally know up there.'

'What if no-one claims him?'

'I suppose he's yours, then.' Charlie grinned at her in the dark. He pulled up outside her house and leaned across to open her door. 'You never know your luck!'

Rowan hopped out. 'Thank you very much for – for what you did.'

'See you in the morning then. I'll pick you up. Say nine-ish.'

'Yes. I'll be ready.'

The Land-Rover turned the corner and went away up the hill. Rowan went in round the back. She could feel herself trembling with excitement and tried to steel herself against her father's bad temper. What if the police let her take the pony and her father wouldn't allow it? She was terrified of the muddle and disappointment that seemed likely to erupt from her evening's adventure. But Charlie — she trusted in Charlie. Utterly. He would see everything came right.

CHAPTER TWO

Charlie came the next morning on the dot of nine. John Watkins had already set off for the garage to see about his damage, so Rowan did not have to explain to him. Her mother was sympathetic, but not very hopeful about Rowan owning a pony.

'It all costs money, Rowan, and we've taken on a big mortgage for this house. Your father won't want it, I know.'

'But if I get it *free*?'

'Oh, come on – pigs might fly! If it's as lovely as you say, someone must be looking for it.'

'Oh, Mum – if – *please*—'

'Let's wait and see what happens.'

Rowan knew she was jumping the gun and getting all tizzed up for something that wasn't going to happen. Concentrate on lovely

Charlie – that was joy enough for one day, to be going out with Charlie. She fetched her anorak and ran out as the Land-Rover rattled to a halt outside her house.

Charlie had the camera.

'We'll see what we've got in the daylight,' he said. He grinned at her, his gypsy-dark eyes full of the joy of living. Rowan had never seen Charlie down, even when his father was nagging him. The Land-Rover was loaded with what looked like half a car.

'You won't mind if I stop off and do a bit of wheeler-dealing at Arnold's? Someone told me he's got some lights that might do for my MG, and I've got an engine he might buy off me which I got for next to nothing at a farm clear-out.'

Charlie was a mechanical whizz and had scraped his own living at mending cars and tractors since leaving school. At school apparently he had been useless, while Josephine had sailed through everything with top marks. Rowan had learned all this from Lizzie. 'What he can do, like ride and mend the horse-box – he can do without, somehow, learning it – it's instinct with him. But Josephine – she's a great rider, but she's really worked at it – had high-powered lessons and everything, and yet when it comes to the push, it's Charlie who can get a horse to do almost anything, more than Josephine. She doesn't say anything, but it makes her mad. Charlie's not interested in competing – Dad makes him, to show off the horses he wants to sell – but really, although he can do it so well, he's not bound up in it like Josephine. I think he wouldn't really bother with horses at all if it wasn't the thing at home. Dad's living, I mean.'

Perhaps Charlie could have mended her father's Mondeo. They pulled up outside the Baileys' farm and walked up the drive into the stockyard. Babar was there, mucking out. Rowan felt her heart banging with excitement again, and tried to pull herself together.

'I've fed 'um,' Babar said. ''E's settled good enough.'

'Great,' said Charlie.

They went into the stable and Rowan peered over the old-fashioned rails of the loose-box. The pony was snatching at a hay-net, and looked round at them nervously. Charlie had the camera with him.

'We'll have to have him outside for the photo.' He explained to Babar what he was doing, and Babar fetched a head-collar. They led the pony out into the yard. Babar held him while Charlie focused the camera. Rowan just stood and stared.

The pony was glorious to her eyes. It was a very dark brown, blue-black across the quarters, like a swallow. Looking at it, Rowan thought suddenly that it must be called Swallow. Swallow for flight, for freedom, for acrobatics, for agility. The pony flung up his head and whinnied loudly, as he had last night, looking in Rowan's direction. He's mine, she thought. Her knees were trembling.

'I bathed his leg,' Babar said. 'It's not bad.'

Charlie examined it. 'It's fine.'

'You think we should let 'um out?'

'No. We'll never catch him again. Keep him in today, till we come back from the police station. We'll call in on the way back.'

Rowan could sense Charlie's meaning: with luck we'll be shot of the problem. He took four photos, and then wrote down the pony's description on a bit of paper, including what Rowan thought were odd characteristics, like the placings of his whorls, where the hair of his coat made little whirlpools here and there, lying in different directions.

'Like his fingerprints, really,' Charlie said. 'They're different on all horses. Mind you, not many people have a note of them anyway, so it doesn't count for much. Freeze-marking's the best security.'

Rowan thought freeze-marking was branding with a number on the horse's back, but didn't like to ask. She was so ignorant. But she had noticed that Lizzie's pony had a number on its back, under where the saddle went. Swallow wasn't freeze-marked.

'I think he ought to be called Swallow,' she said, as they took him back into the loose-box.

'Why not?' said Charlie. 'Short and sweet.'

They said goodbye to Babar and drove off up the village street.

'She's a good kid, Babar,' Charlie remarked. 'Pity about her awful pony. But she only hacks about, and it's OK for that, I suppose. They all make fun of her in the Pony Club, and yet she knows more than most of 'em put together. She'd make a good vet.'

'A vet?' Rowan's smart school in London had said you had to be super-powered to get into veterinary school.

Charlie said, 'It's not only brain you need for a vet. You need to have an instinct for an animal, especially a horse. Babar thinks horse.'

Rowan thought, I think horse. But she didn't know anything at all.

'What's the Pony Club?'

Perhaps that was where you learned.

'Oh, it's a lark for the kiddies. Earnest ladies have you trotting round in circles watching your diagonals. I hated it but Josephine loved it, so do Lizzie and Hugh and them. Lots of competitions and you go to camp and have midnight feasts. That bit's all right.'

'Can anybody go?'

'If you join, and have a pony to ride, yes.'

What bliss, Rowan thought! If she had Swallow . . .

They climbed up out of the valley and past the spot where the pony had appeared out of the blue. Rowan saw the headlamp glass glinting in the verge. She could not think about anything save the pony. It was as if he had bewitched her.

'Is he valuable, do you think?'

'He's the sort – by the look of him – who would be a real winner with a tough rider. But not many kids can handle a strong pony like that. Most people want quiet, safe ponies for their kiddy-winkies, not tearaways. But if he is well-mannered and doesn't tank off, then, yes, I'd say he was worth a bit. He's very well-made. And only six.'

'Someone's bound to be looking for him!'

'You'd think so.'

But when they got into town and found the right man in the police station, it appeared there was no record of a missing pony.

'We know about him, mind you. He's been reported as a danger to traffic several times, once on the motorway. It's a wonder he hasn't caused a bad accident, or got himself killed by now. Have you got the facilities to keep him for the time being, while we make enquiries?'

'Yes.' Charlie produced his paper with drawings of the pony's white markings and the distribution of his whorls. He wrote Rowan's name and address on the bottom.

'She found him.' He gave her a wink. 'It's hers, if no-one claims it.'

'I think we'll probably place him. We'll be in touch with the Horse Watch people, and put the description out. Mind you, some people abandon ponies, like they do dogs and cats, but they're generally poor clapped-out things they can't sell.'

'Oh, he's not like that,' Rowan said quickly.

'No, he's a decent animal,' Charlie said. 'Been well looked after, by the look of him.'

'We'll be in touch. Quite soon if we're lucky.'

They took their leave and went back to the Land-Rover.

'That's that done. We'll go to Arnold's now and see if I can sell him this junk. I've got a living to make.'

Rowan went into a dream of owning Swallow and riding him in competitions against Hugh and Lizzie. Life was going to be unbearable, waiting to hear from the police station.

'You might hear by tonight. They've got it all on computer these days,' Charlie said, scotching her dreams.

He drove quite fast, but carefully in the country lanes, in case someone was riding a horse round the next bend. 'Could be me,' he grinned. 'Josephine got shunted up the rear a couple of years ago, and the horse had to be put down.'

Suppose they had hit Swallow really hard and killed him, Rowan thought! And he'd been on the motorway . . .

'Traffic and horses don't mix any more.

32

When I was little, I rode everywhere and it was perfectly safe, but now—' Charlie shrugged. 'Now a driver will give you the V sign with two fingers. You give it him back and he sees it in his mirror and he'll stop and get out and come back. I've had that.'

'What did you do?'

'I just rode at him. He fell in the ditch. I took his number, in case. They don't understand.'

Rowan thought, secretly, her father might do that. He was always in a hurry and quick-tempered. It made them edgy at home. Her mother was a worrier and tried to keep the peace. She was always saying, 'Your father works so hard, he can't help it.' Charlie's father worked hard too and he was fairly bad-tempered. He shouted, but the next minute he was laughing, so it wasn't too bad.

Arnold's dump was an eyesore tacked onto the edge of a pretty village. There were some decrepit barns and a field full of nettles and ragwort and a thin horse grazing, with a strand of barbed wire keeping it off Arnold's impressive collection of broken-down cars. Charlie drove in and hooted.

'Sorry about this, it shouldn't take too long.'

Charlie hopped out and went to meet a

young man who came out of the barn to meet him.

Rowan sat in the cab waiting. She watched the thin horse cropping the weedy grass and thought how poorly it compared with her gorgeous Swallow. She was impatient to get home and go back to Babar's and see how he was getting on. The thin horse looked like the sort the policeman said people abandoned. It was a chestnut with a white streak down its nose. As she watched it Rowan noticed that it had some dreadful cuts on its back legs, some of which were oozing pus and blood. It needed Babar. Charlie had glanced at the horse, before going to the back of the Land-Rover to unload his junk. Arnold came to help him. Rowan could hear them haggling. Then Arnold said he would go and fetch his price book, whatever that was. When he had disappeared Charlie went over to the wire fence and stood looking at the horse. It came over to him and he took hold of its nose and looked at its teeth.

Rowan got out of the cab. 'What are you doing?'

'I know this horse,' Charlie said. 'I'm looking at its teeth – see how old it is.'

'It's a terrible old horse.'

'She was a good horse once. Fedora. She's only nine.'

She looked like a knacker's horse. When Arnold came back he said she was for the knacker's. Waiting for the lorry to come.

Charlie said, 'You can have this engine in exchange for the horse.'

Arnold did not blink. 'Done,' he said.

They set about transferring the engine out of the Land-Rover and onto a fork-lift truck. Rowan sat, pop-eyed at the transaction. So casual. The mare was still cropping the grass, unaware that she had been saved from the jaws of death. She was tall and skinny, with her ribs showing, yet her belly underneath was fat. She was a bright chestnut, with a raggedy red mane and tail. She had dull eyes, and a resigned demeanour, as if used to hard times.

Charlie came back and they drove off. The Land-Rover felt light and bouncy, having been delivered of its burden.

'Have you got a bargain?' Rowan asked.

'You never know, with a horse.'

'It doesn't look worth much to me.'

'No. She's starving and full of worms. But she's in foal, by the look of her. And she had a good owner a year ago, a man with sense enough to send her to a good stallion. So it could be a good foal. But he died, and his horses were sold.'

'And she fell on bad days?'

'Yes, and got hung up in a barbed-wire fence. The owner's an ignorant fool who bought a nice thoroughbred and ruined it. She was a racehorse, and ex-racehorses don't often make quiet hacks for ignorant people.'

'I want Swallow to be a good hack for an ignorant person.'

Charlie laughed.

'Good, class horses are rare, believe me.'

But Rowan could see that, inside, Charlie was excited by his sudden deal, although he was trying not to show it. She sensed that he was a bit like her with Swallow. On to a dream . . . what might be.

'What will you do with her?'

'Point-to-point her, with luck. She's fast.' Then he added, 'Dad won't be pleased.'

Like hers. 'Why not?'

'He wants me to ride the yard horses – the ones for sale. Get them mannered. If I've got my own, I haven't as much time for his.'

'Does he pay you? Employ you, sort of?'

'You must be joking! Employ me, yes. Pay me, no. That's why I muck about with machinery.'

So Charlie had parent problems too. It made Rowan happy to think she had a bond with Charlie. She wriggled with excitement. All the things to think of . . .

They stopped at the Baileys' farm.

'Will you tell Babar what happened? I want to get the trailer and go back to fetch that mare. If the knacker lorry gets there first it'll take her, I'm sure.'

'Yes, of course.'

Rowan hopped out and Charlie roared off. Rowan went into the stockyard. There was a crashing noise coming from the stable. A loud and unmistakable whinny rent the air. Rowan hurried anxiously into the stable.

There was no sign of Babar, and Black Diamond's box was empty. But Swallow was rampaging round his box, dripping with sweat, and letting fly with his heels at the walls.

'Whatever's the matter?' Rowan was shocked at the pony's distress.

When he saw her he came up to the door, letting out his wild whinnies. He kicked the door with his front feet. His bad knee was swollen up again and he had hollows in his flanks. His coat was wet all over.

Rowan could see that something was wrong but had no idea what. She wished Charlie had come in. He would know. Or Babar. Perhaps Babar was in the house. She decided to go and find her. But as she went out of the yard she met Ted Bailey coming in on his tractor. She waited while he parked it. He got down and smiled at her.

'That little beggar'll 'ave my stable down. 'Ark at 'im!' He didn't seem to mind.

'What's wrong with him?'

''E'll be all right when Barbara comes back. She's gone for a ride, and 'e's missing the other pony, like.'

Was that all? Rowan was amazed.

'Did the police know anything about 'um?' (So that's where Babar got the 'um from.)

'No. But they're going to find out.'

'Ah well. I daresay they'll come up with sommat.'

'Is it all right, him being here with you?' What if he threw him out for attacking his stable?

But Ted Bailey was a patient, affable man, nothing like John Watkins and Fred Hawes.

'Oh, aye, 'e's no trouble. 'E can bide 'ere till they find 'is owner.'

'That's very kind of you.'

He went off towards the cowshed and Rowan was left with a panic that perhaps, because he was looking after him, he might claim the pony if the police didn't come up with an owner. He might want him for Babar! Anyone with any sense would prefer Swallow to Black Diamond. While she stood there worrying, Babar rode into the yard. She wore her brown anorak and green gumboots for riding, just the same as for everything, but she had added a hard hat, without bothering to cover its uncompromising grey surface with the usual jolly silk. As soon as Swallow saw Black Diamond he stood still and stopped whinnying.

'I know 'e was upset, but 'e's got to learn, same as all,' Babar said. 'I can't not ride, 'cause of 'um.'

She lumbered down from the saddle and led Diamond into his box. Swallow was now all happy little whickering noises, his kicking forgotten. Rowan was amazed.

'What did the police say?' Babar asked, as she unsaddled Diamond.

Rowan told her. 'Do you think they'll find the owner?'

'Likely.'

Babar took off the bridle and kissed Diamond several times on the nose. He stood with his eyes shut, breathing heavily. He had long, lop ears, which tended to fall out sideways, and his neck was concave along the top instead of convex.

Rowan, unable to bear the anxiety of perhaps Ted Bailey claiming him, said, 'I do hope they don't! I would love to keep him.'

Babar lifted her large round face from Diamond's nose and looked at her with surprise.

'Keep 'um? You?'

'Yes!'

'You don't know . . . you never . . .' She stopped.

'Would you want him?' Rowan blurted out.

'Me?' Babar laughed. 'What would I want 'um for, when I got my darling 'ere?'

The great weight lifted from Rowan and she laughed too. 'Oh, I would so love to have him! More than anything I can think of! I would so love to have a pony.'

'A pony, yes. But this one? You don't know nothin'.' This was spoken quite kindly, as a fact, not with scorn.

'I could learn!'

'You got to learn with a pony as'll teach you.'

Rowan thought people taught, not ponies. She was out of her depth. She did not want to show any more of her ignorance and knew it was time to go home for lunch, or her parents would be worrying. She looked at her watch.

'I must go. Shall I come back and help you look after Swallow later?'

'Swallow?'

'I've called him Swallow.'

'Oh aye. Well, 'e's mucked out for today. You could come up in the morning and do 'im, if you want.'

'What time?'

'Six-thirty, say.'

Rowan flinched. What would her mother say! 'Yes, all right. And thank-you – thank-you for looking after him.'

Babar gave her a puzzled look, from which Rowan surmised that people like the Baileys always looked after an animal if it was there, under their noses, and it was not something to be thanked for. Babar made her feel incredibly suburban. Babar came with her out of the stockyard carrying her saddle and bridle. As they did so there was a clatter of hooves on the lane outside and a girl about their own age rode past on a gleaming bay pony. The girl wore bright cross-country clothes with a matching silk and the pony had bandages and boots to match. The pair were as unlike the Bailey turnout as it was possible to be.

'Who's that?' Rowan asked, as the girl passed on – having glanced in with stony eyes and made no greeting.

'That's Matty Prebble. She lives at High Bottom.' And then, in a tone of ineffable scorn – 'Show-jumper.'

CHAPTER THREE

'So, did you find out who owned that pony?'

Rowan scrambled home just in time for lunch and her mother asked the leading question.

'No. But the police will ring here if they find the owner.'

'So whose is it at the moment?' her father asked.

'Mine.' Rowan heard her own voice quiver with defiance. Her mother darted her an anxious look.

'And you are paying for its food and keep?'

'Well, Mr Bailey hasn't said anything about that. He doesn't mind having it there.'

'They're a hard bunch when it comes to money, these farmers.' As far as Rowan was aware her father didn't know any farmers. He certainly had made no steps to be friendly with

Mr Bailey and Mr Flint. Mr Bailey hadn't struck Rowan as hard. Soft, she would have said, to the point of squelchiness.

'Mr Bailey's not hard. He said I could keep it there. Or I could keep it at High Hawes.'

'The question doesn't arise, save for a day or two until the police find the owner.'

'But if they don't—'

'They must have an arrangement for disposing of such animals.'

'Charlie said they just want to get shot of them. I could have it, Charlie said. For my own.'

'That's out of the question.'

'It would be *free*,' Rowan cried, picking on the most likely attraction for her father. 'And he's valuable. Charlie said so. Only six and very nicely made. We'd get a valuable pony for nothing.'

'Hmm. If it's that valuable, someone is bound to be looking for it.'

But he didn't exactly say she couldn't have it. Rowan was clever enough to change the subject at this point.

'I saw a girl called Matty Prebble who lives at High Bottom. She's a show-jumper.'

Although Babar had sounded so scornful,

Rowan had been impressed with her glimpse of Matty Prebble. She hoped she would grow up more like Matty than Babar.

Her mother said, 'Oh, I've met Mrs Prebble. She's very smart. Outspoken. Her husband's in a merchant bank.'

When Rowan went up to High Hawes after lunch and mentioned Matty Prebble to Hugh, he crossed his eyes and made being-sick noises.

'Yuk!'

'What's that mean?'

'She thinks she's so wonderful! They spend thousands on her show-jumpers. All she has to do is ride them. Any fool could do that.'

Hugh was in the stable saddling up his pony Cascade. Cascade was a tough-looking flea-bitten grey of about fourteen hands, rather the same build as Swallow, but not so pretty. Cascade had cost almost nothing, being considered unrideable by the poor disillusioned children who had struggled with him during his chequered former career. Most of the Hawes children's ponies were cast-outs picked up for a song by their father. The Hawes's combined expertise nearly always reformed them, and then they were sold on for a lot of money. But

45

Cascade, according to Hugh, was not for sale. He adored Cascade.

'I bet *she* couldn't get this one round a set of show-jumps,' he said scathingly. 'For all she thinks she's so marvellous.'

'Can you?'

'Of course.'

Rowan wished she hadn't asked. Unlike Charlie, Hugh was a bit prickly at times, no doubt by having to keep his end up amongst his siblings and handicapped by being nearly the youngest. He had a competitive nature, and was very strong for his age (eleven) and could unload hay bales like a grown man. He was fair, a scalped blond, with bright blue eyes, finely-chiselled features and a naturally worried expression. Rowan liked him and rather admired him. He was in the same class as her at school and was quite clever.

'Charlie says you've got yourself a pony,' he remarked, pulling up Cascade's girth. He kept his elbow well out to fend off as the pony turned round to bite him. 'He says it's nice.'

'Only until it's claimed.'

'It might not be. If it's trouble, someone might rather have the insurance money.'

'Charlie says it looks valuable.'

'Charlie's potty. That horse he got this morning – Dad's furious. It's rubbish. Dad says he won't have it in his yard.'

'Why ever not?'

'He doesn't like Charlie acting off his own bat. He wants Charlie to work on the yard horses, not have one of his own. He's mad now, but he'll cool down later. He's like that.'

What a liability parents were, Rowan thought!

'What will Charlie do, if he can't bring the mare back here?'

'He's going to put it in with Bailey's cows for the time being.'

Rowan decided to go down to the Baileys' to see the homecoming. Charlie had gone off in the horse-box an hour ago and it was to meet him coming back with his mare that she had come up to High Hawes. She was in the wrong place.

Hugh led Cascade out of his loose-box and hopped on without using the stirrup. They made a good pair, Rowan thought – two of a kind – strong and bossy and handsome. She fetched her bike and they rode out of the yard together. Above the farm the lane led up into some woods and above that to the open down where one could ride for miles. On the other side were racehorse gallops and in the next valley several racing stables. Hugh went uphill and Rowan went down. She whizzed down to the village, thinking how lucky she was to have High Hawes so close, and all its interesting, warring factions. She braked as she came to the village street, turned right past her own house (her father was mowing the lawn and did not look up) and pedalled furiously up to the Baileys'. The High Hawes horse-box was in the drive and Charlie was just getting out of the cab.

'Hi, trouble,' he said. 'My dad's furious with you.'

'Whatever for?' Rowan was startled.

'Not stopping me buying this mare. Anyone with any sense, he said, would have pointed out what a stupid idea it was. He's refused to let me bring her home.'

'Yes. Hugh just told me.'

Charlie laughed. 'All for the best. I thought we could turn 'em out together – yours and mine. A mare for a companion should keep your little beast happy. Stop him jumping out.'

He let down the back ramp and pulled down the slatted doors. The chestnut mare looked down on them with her resigned expression.

'No, it's not the knacker's. Lucky old you,' Charlie said to her. He led her down the ramp and into the stockyard and tied her up outside the stables. From inside Swallow let out one of his loud whinnies. Rowan was drawn to the door, to see his bright flashing eyes regarding her through the rails of his loose-box. If only he were really hers! She would look as happy as Charlie. It was obvious that his father's wrath was not deterring him.

Babar came out and admired the mare, and fetched some hot water from the kitchen, a basin, and cotton-wool to bathe the mare's legs. She and Charlie crouched down, heads touching, to examine the cuts and Rowan knew she was only a spectator. She wandered back to the stable and stood absorbing the atmosphere, sniffing the pleasant smell of horse and fresh hay. She had fallen in love with this world, she realized. Even before Swallow, she had been drawn to High Hawes by its peculiar dedication to the routine imposed by a stableful of horses: it gave a sense of purpose and stability and absorbed the frustrations that Rowan had become familiar with in her old suburban life – what to do, where to go . . . there was no time to be bored. It was very physical and outdoor, and yet there were intriguing problems, she had noticed, which required brain and cunning and the innate horse-sense which she recognized in Charlie and Babar and Hugh, and which she guessed she would never learn however hard she tried. Horse-sense — it was a description that had transcended the horse world and was used in everyday life. She wished dearly that she had it.

Black Diamond, covered with his old jute rug, stood munching hay in his corner, not looking up, while Swallow paced round his box, excited by the goings-on outside. Rowan stroked him, but he would not respond to her fondling, but jerked away and whinnied again.

'What's wrong with him?' she asked Charlie.

'Nothing.'

'Your horses don't all whinny and stamp about.'

'They would if they'd been running wild for a couple of weeks, been out on the motorway, hit by a car, lost their own home and friends and been shut up in a strange place all of a sudden.'

Rowan digested this. It made sense.

'It takes time,' Charlie said. 'Horses are

creatures of habit. They like their routine. The same every day. Otherwise they get upset. Your pony is upset, that's all. Nothing is wrong.'

'Not like this 'un,' said Babar darkly. 'Them legs—' She shrugged.

'They will heal.'

'Knacker's next week instead o' this,' said Babar.

'Oh, come on!' Charlie looked uneasy. 'She'll win. Everything's oozing beautifully.'

'Poison.'

'I want to put her out. I believe in nature. It's cleaner out.'

'Dad said you can use the Thin Acre.'

'Good. That'll suit her fine. I thought Rowan's pony could go out with her, might settle him.'

'Yeah, good idea.'

'Suppose he jumps out again?' Rowan asked anxiously.

'He won't,' they both said together.

How did they know, Rowan wondered?

Babar fetched a head-collar and led Swallow out. He came with a rush, ears pricked, hooves skidding. His coat almost glittered in the pale spring sunshine, the blue cast on his back giving way to brownish lights round his eyes and mouth. Charlie's poor mare lifted up her head and pricked her ears with interest, her nostrils rippling. Swallow let out one of his loud neighs.

'Give over!' said Babar. Then to Rowan, with a sly smile, 'D'you want him? 'E's yours.'

Charlie looked worried. 'Hang on, whatever you do.'

Rowan took the rope from Babar, very nervous.

Charlie said to her, 'You take the mare.'

He handed her the mare's head rope and took Swallow, without asking her. Rowan was relieved, rather than upset.

The Thin Acre was up the road about a hundred yards, on the opposite side from the farm. The field lay alongside the lane, long and thin as its name implied, sloping down to a stream on the far side. It was surrounded with high, rampant hedges and trees and the grass was long and sweet. Babar, going ahead, opened the gate and Rowan led the mare through first. She put her head down before she was half through the opening and started to tear at the good grass. Charlie barged past, half dragged by Swallow, and Babar, shoving

Fedora's quarters out of the way, closed the gate.

'Let her go. Leave the head-collar on,' Charlie said.

Rowan unclipped the rope. The mare made no move to explore but just stood cropping greedily, while Swallow, released, galloped up to the top of the field. Rowan was petrified he would go through the hedge, but it was thick and high and he stopped with a great tearing of hooves in the turf, flung himself round and galloped back right down to the bottom end. They all stood watching.

'Cor, he can move!' Charlie said.

Infected by the pony's exuberance, Fedora suddenly put up her old head with a toss of the raggedy mane and cantered a few paces after him, before the wounds in her hind legs suggested it would be better to desist – just enough to show the lovely, smooth action of the good thoroughbred. For a moment, she looked beautiful. Even Rowan, tearing her gaze from Swallow, could see it.

'She's not a bad 'un, moving,' Babar said stolidly.

'I tell you, she's a really good mare. I

remember her winning at Newbury. Dad wouldn't believe me.'

They leaned on the gate in a row, watching the two animals. Swallow settled down quite quickly and started to graze, keeping very close to the mare. Rowan thought of the mare, destined for the knacker's, being waylaid in the nick of time and turned out into what she obviously thought was paradise, and tears came into her eyes. And Swallow – finding this good home and a friend . . . it wasn't just herself who found the sight satisfying, for Charlie was in no hurry to go home.

Babar said, 'You needn't keep coming down. I'll see to her legs – tonight, like, and in the morning.'

'I'll come down if I can. But knowing Dad, he'll find me plenty to do.'

Rowan wasn't sure if she had to do anything. She didn't know if horses just stayed out, or whether you had to feed them or anything. She didn't like to ask. She noticed that on the far side of the stream the field sloped up to the house of the Prebbles, High Bottom. Where the ground levelled out at the top there was an enclosure full of show jumps where no doubt Matty Prebble did her practising. Matty Prebble would have horse sense, like Babar and Charlie.

'A good day's work,' Charlie said, as they walked back up the road. He closed up the back of the horse-box and climbed up into the cab. Babar saw the lorry out into the road and Charlie drove away. Rowan had no excuse to linger, although she wondered if she should offer to clean out Swallow's stable again. She offered, and Babar said it didn't matter, so Rowan fetched her bike and rode home.

Having Swallow out in the field just down the road made it very easy for her to visit. She went down with titbits the moment she got home from school and both horses would come to the gate and nuzzle at her as she groped in her pockets. Fedora's legs started to heal nicely. Swallow stopped whinnying and galloping about and worrying, and started to look the model of a quiet, safe pony. Every day Rowan expected her mother to say she had heard from the police, but nothing happened. Monday, Tuesday, Wednesday, Thursday . . . Rowan became more and more optimistic.

Friday.

She burst into the kitchen, throwing off her school blazer and scrummaging in the bread-bin for crusts, and her mother came through from the dining-room and said, 'Oh, a man rang this afternoon. He said the police had given him our number. That pony you found – he thinks it's his. He's coming over in the morning.'

CHAPTER FOUR

Rowan's father decided to accompany Rowan to meet the man who thought Swallow was his. The man had arranged to call at the farm at eleven o'clock. Rowan had wished Charlie would come, and thought perhaps Mr Bailey might take an interest, but on Saturday morning there was only Babar in the yard when she went down.

She told Babar what had happened. She had come down an hour ahead of her father, to talk to Swallow before he might disappear. She could not stop a few tears falling out when she told Babar; but Babar, for all she was commonsensical, was not scornful.

'You got fond of 'um. It's a shame.'

Rowan tried to cheer herself up by picturing a lovely family arriving and falling on Swallow with exclamations of delight, and

Swallow whinnying back to them with love and affection. But why had they taken so long? Perhaps they had been on holiday. But it was a bit early for holiday time.

'Will you come and meet them, at eleven o'clock?'

She was nervous of catching Swallow by herself, and revealing how awkward she was with ponies in front of her father. But perhaps when Swallow caught sight of his erstwhile owners he would canter over and plunge his nose into their hands full of titbits.

It was a cold, miserable day. Rowan had a feeling everything was going to go wrong. She hated the idea of her father coming down and saying all the wrong things to these people. He had no idea. The man was called Mr Harvey, the police said. He was able to describe the pony exactly, right down to a wire scar on the off hind fetlock. Rowan had never noticed this herself and nor had Charlie.

Babar finished grooming Black Diamond and they went down to the field together. The two animals were grazing down by the stream. When he saw them Swallow lifted his head, ears pricked, and started to walk over, and Charlie's mare followed, but more slowly. Watching them, Rowan was choked with disappointment. She told herself she had only known Swallow a week, and not to be so stupid. But when he came close his nostrils rippled a greeting and he came to her like an old friend. Rowan howled.

'Your dad's coming,' Babar said anxiously.

The Mondeo was pulling up on the verge. Rowan blew her nose hastily. Her father got out and came marching up.

'So this is the fellow?' He put out a hand and pulled it back hastily as Swallow reached towards it, thinking it held something nice. 'It's very good of your father to take it in,' he said to Babar.

Babar looked at him with disdain, obviously wondering what else he would have done. Shooed it off down the road? She did not reply.

John Watkins looked at his watch. 'I hope he's not going to keep us waiting. I've got work to do.'

Rowan was used to her father's impatience. He didn't really have any work to do, save clean the car and mow the lawn, as far as she knew, not like Mr Bailey who had a hundred and twenty cows to milk twice a day, as well as make hay and grow corn. Yet Mr Bailey was never impatient. Rowan knew her father charged his clients an enormous sum by the hour. If Ted Bailey charged by the hour he would be a millionaire. But he had no-one to charge. Life was very unfair.

But before her father had time to get cross, a car came down the road from the top, pulling a horse trailer. Rowan was shocked by seeing the trailer. This man must be quite sure! The car slowed down by the gate and the driver put his head out of the window. He was quite young, wore a tweed cap, and had a rather ferretty face. There was no doting family with him; he was alone.

'Are you—?'

'Watkins. John Watkins. Got your pony, I believe?' Rowan's father sprang forward. Rowan thought he sounded as if he couldn't wait to get Swallow loaded up.

'So I understand. Can I park somewhere?'

'In the drive.' Babar gestured down the road towards the farm.

He drove on and into the farmyard, and came back on foot, carrying a head-collar. He wore jodhpurs and was rather bandy, like a jockey. He did not look like a kind father looking for his darling daughter's lost pony, which was rather what Rowan had been expecting.

He introduced himself. 'Ken Harvey. The police tell me our fellow's been here a week or so now. I've been away, I'm afraid. Only heard last night.'

'This is the one. I take it he's yours?'

Ken Harvey took a cursory glance at Swallow and said, 'That's the fellow. Cornhill Amethyst – my daughter's show-pony.'

His eyes flicked quickly over Swallow. He went up to him and put his head-collar on him, but Swallow did not nuzzle him happily as Rowan had been expecting. In fact he stepped back and put back his ears. But Ken Harvey was obviously experienced at handling ponies and brooked no nonsense.

John Watkins, perhaps sensing that it was all too easy, said, 'I take it you can identify him in some way?'

'Yes, of course. I think you'll find he's got a small scar on his hind fetlock, near side. Shaped like a star. Want to have a look? Six years old – have you looked in his mouth? And, if you look under his mane, off side, there are some white hairs in his coat, just a few.'

Rowan had never noticed. She lifted up the mane and looked. It was true. There were. She felt bitterly disappointed. She felt the tears rising up again and turned away. Babar opened the gate and Ken Harvey led the pony out. Fedora came to the gate and looked sadly after them, and gave a soft whinny. Swallow turned his head and bellowed in reply. Ken Harvey chucked at his head.

'What do I owe you, for keep for a week?'

'Nothing,' said Babar. 'It's only grass.'

Rowan's father said, 'There will be an insurance claim, I'm afraid, for damage to my car. Your animal jumped out of a hedge in front of me and my headlight was broken. Perhaps you'll give me the particulars of your insurance, and your address?'

'Certainly. We'll box him up and I'll give you my card. I'll sort it out with the insurance.'

Babar let down the ramp of the trailer and Harvey led Swallow in. Rowan went to the front and went in by the groom's door to Swallow's front end, and let herself cry in the soft gloom while the two men talked outside. Swallow licked her hands and she kissed the softness of his muzzle.

'I don't like your Mr Harvey,' she said. She

had wanted a jolly father and a nice girl with loving eyes and a white-toothed smile, who would write her letters later on, and invite her home for weekends. Not a bandy-legged jockey with a ferretty face.

'Come on, Rowan,' her father called.

She retreated. It was awful. She didn't care who saw her crying now. She ran away from them and got into her father's car and sobbed. She heard her father directing the man out into the village street, and then the acceleration as the car drove away, and thought she heard a last faint whinny. Her father came back to the car.

'Bit of luck, that. Looks as if I shall get my insurance claim.'

Rowan was so angry at her father's callous remark that she jumped out of the car and ran back to Babar's stable. Babar understood, at least. She was going to go for a ride but she stopped tacking up when she saw Rowan and stood there looking sympathetic.

'He was horrible!' Rowan cried out.

'Aye.'

'And my father's horrible too! All he's bothered about is his beastly insurance money!'

'Aye.'

'I did want to keep Swallow. I really wanted to!'

'Perhaps your dad would let you have a pony, all the same, if you want one.'

'I only want Swallow!'

Rowan knew she was behaving like an infant child but she couldn't help herself. It was all right with Babar. If Charlie had been there she would have tried to be more sensible.

'I'm sorry,' she mumbled. 'I know I'm being stupid. It's just that he was such a horrid man.'

Babar said, 'He was that. Jus' took it for granted. No thanks.'

'No. He never said thank-you at all! Or even looked pleased.'

'An' the pony didn't know him, like.'

'What do you mean?'

'Looked like it to me, when he put the head-collar on – the pony seemed like he thought 'e was a stranger.'

'Yes, he did!' Rowan was alarmed at what Babar was hinting. 'You think he — he—'

'I wouldna' trust 'um myself. Not farther than I could throw 'um. But 'e knew the pony's marks, 'is age and everything . . .' She shrugged.

'My father's got his card, his address. I don't see how he could cheat us.'

'No. Right. 'E just smelled like a wrong 'un.'

'Yes, he did.'

Rowan could see that Babar wanted to be off on her ride so she retreated and walked slowly home. Babar's remarks had set her thinking. She asked her father if she could see the card the man had given her, and he said it was on the mantelpiece, why?

'I just want to see where he lives. If it's near.'

She copied down the address. It was the same county but she had no idea where it was. She wrote down the telephone number. She wanted to talk to Charlie. After lunch she got her bike and toiled up to High Hawes. The yard was empty, so she knocked at the kitchen door.

'Come in!' someone yelled.

The Hawes family were sitting down to lunch in the kitchen. Joan Hawes was lobbing hot cheese rarebits out of the grill, apparently ready to go on until nobody wanted any more, and eating one herself as she worked. Rowan was embarrassed, having thought lunch-time would be over, but nobody minded and Joan Hawes did one for her too. Lizzie and Hugh budged up at the table and let her in, without seeming cross about it, and Charlie grinned at her from across the table.

'Someone came for Swallow. He says he's his and has taken him away.'

Charlie's grin vanished. 'Oh, bad luck!'

'Wow, that's quick,' Hugh said.

'The police rang last night. And he came with a trailer this morning.'

'What, just like that? How did he know, without looking first?'

'He knew all his marks, scars and things. He was horrid. Really horrid.' She was afraid she might burst into tears again and picked up her cheesy toast.

'Who was he? Anyone we know?'

'Ken Harvey.'

'Rings no bells.'

'I knew a Ken Harvey, years ago,' Fred Hawes said. 'A jockey. Crook. Got banned.'

'He looked like a jockey. He looked like a ferret.'

'Yeah, like a ferret.'

None of this was at all cheering to Rowan.

66

Only Charlie guessed how she felt and he, being practical, was concerned for Fedora, left on her own.

'She'll be better off up here. I'll fetch her this afternoon.' He looked cautiously at his father, who shrugged and said, 'She'll have to go out with the youngsters. If they run her round . . . it's up to you.'

'She'll be OK. She's not flighty.'

Fred shook his head, but did not argue. He was a thick-set, tough-looking man with a lined face but surprisingly gentle eyes. Horses would do anything for him, Babar had told Rowan. The magic had rubbed off on Charlie. But Fred found humans difficult to handle and was not as successful as he should have been. High Hawes was not in debt, but there was no spare cash for a new horse-box or a good eventer for the ambitious Josephine. Josephine was going to have to make her own eventer out of one of the bargain youngsters bought on a trip to Ireland. It was her job, and Charlie's, to break them in. Josephine was nothing like Charlie, being very quiet and cold by nature. She kept herself very much to herself, but missed nothing with her clear, blue-grey eyes. If she had done anything to enhance her looks, she would have been strikingly beautiful, Rowan thought, in awe of her. She was working for her Pony Club A test, which Rowan understood from Hugh and Lizzie was phenomenally difficult to pass.

After lunch Rowan went out into the yard with Hugh and Lizzie who were going for a ride.

She was so transparently miserable that Lizzie said, 'If we had something quiet to ride, you could have a go. But we haven't. When we come back you could ride Cascade up the lane, I suppose. If Hugh leads him.'

'I don't mind,' said Hugh obligingly.

'It doesn't matter,' Rowan said. It really didn't, just then. She didn't want to ride another pony. Only Swallow.

She went with Lizzie to tack up Lizzie's pony Birdie. Birdie was a bay, almost thorough-bred, of fourteen and a half hands, a lean and beautiful mare with a wilful nature. Her proper name was Bird in the Wilderness. She had been christened by a woman called Mrs Brundle who had 'rescued' her. Mrs Brundle had given her to Lizzie. The Hawes called Mrs Brundle Mrs Bundle, because she looked like one, her terrible old clothes tied round the middle with a piece of binder twine. She lived alone in an ancient house at the opposite end of the village from the Baileys and was thought to be eccentric but harmless, a collector of unwanted dogs, cats, goats, donkeys and ponies and injured hedgehogs, owls, orphan fox-cubs and one-winged pheasants. She was elderly and said to be an Honourable something, but looked like a bag-lady. The Hawes said she was all right. Batty but all right.

Lizzie was never convinced that being given Birdie was a good thing. Her father said it was, naturally, but Birdie was very hard to get on with.

'Charlie schools her for me when I get desperate. She's all right with him.'

'Desperate?' Rowan was surprised.

Lizzie had her head down, groping under the pony's belly for her girth. She mumbled, 'She can be awfully silly, you can't imagine. She was spoilt as a youngster and doesn't understand obvious things, like obedience. Nobody taught her. I'm having to do it, about three years too late.'

'Is it hard work?'

Lizzie's head popped up over the saddle and her blue eyes looked sharply at Rowan.

'It's not very easy, no. It's all right for the

others – Charlie and Hugh – and even Shrimp
– she's only nine but she's got no nerves at
all – but I'm not as good as the rest of them.
Hugh's better than I am and he's *two years
younger*. I hate not being as good as him, you
can't imagine.'

Rowan was surprised at the sudden misery
in Lizzie's voice. She always thought Lizzie
looked marvellous on her pony. Lizzie was
small and thin with rather wild curly hair
which sprang out spectacularly when she took
her riding hat off. She was rather scatty and
impulsive by nature, unlike Charlie and Hugh.
Perhaps horses preferred calm natures, Rowan
thought; it seemed logical. If Birdie was scatty
too, it might not be a good mix.

'Why can't your father sell her and let you
have something easier?'

'He's going to. She's got a fabulous jump
and the idea is to sell her to Matty Prebble. Mrs
Prebble wants her, but Dad's holding out. He
likes annoying Mrs Prebble. And I'm supposed
to be improving Birdie, so he can get more
money.'

'Mrs Brundle won't mind?'

'Not as long as she goes to a good home.
Dad's already discussed it with her. I suppose

he'll give her some of the money.'

Lizzie led the pony out into the yard and Rowan followed. How complicated this pony business seemed to be! Rowan was impressed by Lizzie's confidences, reassured by finding that she wasn't the only one with problems. Being an only child, she had never considered how competitive it must be having four brothers and sisters to be compared with.

'I'll muck out while you're away,' she said, to be helpful.

'You haven't got to. You could fetch Fedora with Charlie.'

So she mucked out their empty loose-boxes and when Charlie came out she walked down with him to fetch Fedora. He too was sympathetic, but had seen so many loved horses whipped from under him to be sold by his father that he took it as a fact of life. 'Someone was bound to turn up for a little cracker like him.'

Fedora was standing by the gate looking as bereft as Rowan.

'Lost your mate, old girl?' Charlie gave her a friendly pat and put the head-collar on. 'She's in foal. I had the vet look at her. He thinks it's due around June. Could be something nice, if we're lucky. I'll try and find out when it's born – what stallion she was sent to – so I can get it registered. She looks better already, doesn't she – a week on good grass?'

Certainly the mare had lost her hang-dog look, and her cuts were healing nicely.

'I can feed her when I get her home. I knew dad would give in.'

They walked back up the hill with the mare between them, and Charlie turned her out with some shaggy two-year-olds. By then Lizzie and Hugh had returned and were unsaddling their ponies.

Lizzie said to Rowan, 'Hugh had an idea. He said that man who took your pony – he might have pinched it – you know, just said it was his.'

'But he knew his markings, his scar and that.'

'Hugh said, if you could be bothered, you could come one night and find his markings, when nobody was about. If you heard that a pony had been found, you see, and asked the police where it was. Hugh said it would be easy.'

'Lots of people knew about him. Babar's father asked around at the market on Wednesday, Babar said.'

'Well, your Mr Harvey could have heard.'

'But he gave us his card. His address and phone number. He can't be a thief.'

'It might be false. People do that.'

'We could ring him up and see!'

'Yes. If it's right and he answers, we can pretend to be those people who want to sell you double glazing.'

'Yes!'

'Another thing, what did you say he said the pony's name was? Cornhill Amethyst?'

'Yes.'

'Because we know a lot about show-ponies and we've never heard of the prefix Cornhill.'

'He made it up!'

Rowan's hunch that Ken Harvey was all wrong was being substantiated. She felt herself filling with excitement. If her father had been swindled, he would be as keen to get the pony back as she was. Such was his nature, he could not bear to be bettered.

'We'll ring him,' Hugh said. 'You've got the number? Come on.'

They shut the stable doors and ran across the yard to the house. It was a cold day, and a lovely warmth hit them as they burst into the kitchen. Joan Hawes was rolling out pastry on the kitchen table and Shrimp was painting a picture of a horse, her tongue sticking out as she concentrated. She was a volatile, very independent child, like Lizzie in looks, small for her age and with an elfin face. Her ears stuck out and she anchored her hair firmly behind the useful holders. Charlie had taught her to ride when she was two and she was phenomenally gifted, even for a Hawes, and was much in demand by owners of small show ponies to show them in the ring. Her photo, hair tightly plaited and tied with red bows, was often in 'Horse and Hound' sitting on a pony decorated with championship ribbons. Delighted owners rewarded her with presents and she had become conceited, according to Lizzie, and revolting. The rest of the family derided showing, unless it involved jumping. Shrimp had so many rides she didn't want a pony of her own – 'All that horrid work – no thank you!'

Hugh looked at her painting and said, 'What's that, a giraffe?' Shrimp kicked him and Hugh pulled her hair out from behind her ears so that she couldn't see him.

'Hugh,' said his mother, quite quietly, and he stopped teasing immediately and said, 'Can we use the phone?'

'What for?'

He explained. Joan Hawes was quite interested and said yes, but be tactful.

Rowan found her heart was pulsing with excitement. 'Do you want to do it?' Hugh asked.

'No!'

'I will,' said Lizzie, and snatched up the receiver. Rowan held out the paper with the number on and Lizzie dialled it.

After a few moments she said, 'It's not ringing. Just making a burring noise.'

'Ring the operator!' Hugh shouted.

Lizzie rang the operator and was told it was a discontinued number. She put the receiver down and they all stared at each other in triumph.

'There, he's a fraud!'

'What about the address?' Hugh snatched the paper.

The address was a farm in a village about twenty miles away.

'I bet it doesn't exist,' Hugh said.

'We know someone in that village,' Lizzie said. 'That girl with the show-jumper called Jiminy Cricket. She lives there. What's her name?'

'Rachel Potterton.'

'Yes. That's it. We could ring her and ask about this farm, Elder's End. If Ken Harvey does live there, she's bound to know him.'

They looked up Potterton in the phone book and found the number. Lizzie rang again. Rachel answered the phone. Lizzie said they were trying to trace someone called Ken Harvey at Elder's End but his phone didn't work. Then she was silent while Rachel apparently chattered away. Then she said, 'No wonder we couldn't get an answer! Thank you very much,' and put the phone down.

'There!' She turned triumphantly to Rowan. 'Elder's End is derelict and no-one has lived there for years. And Rachel's never heard of Ken Harvey. So he is a thief!'

Rowan's mind whirled. 'But where's Swallow now? Where's he taken him?'

'He'll sell him on the market. That's what horse thieves do. For cats' meat!'

CHAPTER FIVE

Rowan wept again and Mrs Hawes gave her a biscuit straight out of the oven. Hugh said they should all have a day off school on Monday to go round the markets. Charlie came in and said to Rowan, 'Of course he won't go for cats' meat, he's too classy,' and they sat round the table arguing about what was to be done.

Fred Hawes came in and said if he saw Ken Harvey again he'd come heavy with him. The only market on Monday was over Porchester way and that was very likely where the pony would turn up, unless Mr Harvey had private customers.

'He's in a strong position, because the real owners seem to have gone missing.'

'Rowan's the real owner,' Hugh said.

'No. Morally, perhaps, but not in law. If Ken Harvey sells this pony on the market, there's no-one to prosecute him if the real owners don't turn up. You could go and explain what's happened to the police on Monday morning but I doubt if they'll trouble to go into it. See it from their point of view. It's not worth their trouble.'

'So what shall we do?'

'Go to market and see if we can see him before he goes in the ring,' said Charlie. 'Then, if Mr Harvey's any sense, he'll melt quietly away and you'll get your pony back.'

'But it's school tomorrow!' Rowan wailed.

'Perhaps your father will go?'

Angry as he might be, Rowan's father was not the sort, Rowan thought, to want to go round a cattle market hassling dubious characters. It wasn't his scene at all. Hassling them in a smart office, in his dark suit and club tie, was a different matter.

'Can't you go?' she whispered to Charlie. 'Ken Harvey'd be frightened of you.'

She wouldn't have dared to have asked him, only it mattered so. He looked dubious, and glanced at his father.

'I could skip school,' Rowan said. 'I'm sure my father would let me, for this.'

She had not underestimated her father's

reaction. He was furious when he heard of the spurious address and non-existent telephone number. Rowan knew it was because he wouldn't get paid for the damage to his car, not really because he had been cheated out of the pony.

'You didn't want the pony anyway,' his wife reminded him.

'I didn't want the pony but I don't like being cheated. The man's a rogue. A real rogue.'

But he refused to take a day off from the office to go and chase him at the market.

'Ask those horsey friends of yours to go. We're laying no claim to the pony. If they catch the fellow, they can keep the pony, as far as I'm concerned.'

'Would you let me off school to go with them?' Rowan asked.

'Well, this once, I might.'

Rowan rang Charlie and told him what her father had said. 'If we find him, you can have the pony, Dad says.'

'It's not his to give.'

'No. But he thinks it is,' Rowan explained.

'Well, it's worth a throw, I suppose. We keep it and no-one claims it for long enough, it'd be ours. I'll ask Dad.'

Fred Hawes said it was up to Charlie, if he wanted to go cavorting round the country on a wild-goose chase. Charlie told Rowan he'd go, and she could come with him. Rowan was sure Charlie only said it to comfort her, because he was so nice. He didn't want to go, she was sure. She felt humbled and warm, because he was so kind, and rather guilty about taking up his time.

But the next morning, when the school bus went off without her, she was excited about the prospect ahead of her, and raced up to High Hawes on her bike. It was a cold but sunny day, and Josephine was already out schooling in the home-built manège that they had tried hard to make horizontal on the side of the hill. (Charlie had dug it out with a borrowed JCB when he was only fifteen, and most of the spoil had been turned into a splendid bank and drop-jump exercise at the far end of the schooling field.) Josephine had a young horse which her father had obtained as part-exchange in a deal, and which he would not sell on – 'I've a reputation to maintain.' It looked perfectly all right to Rowan. She did not know about these things. Josephine rode with total concentration, her pale face expressionless beneath the hard grey hat. Her slender body and long, long legs looked brilliant on the thoroughbred. But Rowan remembered with a little leap of joy that Charlie was better – Lizzie had said so. She found herself blushing as Charlie appeared out of the tack shed and gave her his cheerful smile. She could not help it.

'Glutton for punishment – that's you! Or do you just want a day off school?'

'I want Swallow.'

'Seriously, don't expect too much. It's only an outside chance that he'll be there.'

'I know. You don't really mind coming, do you?'

'No. I like a day out occasionally.'

'Mum gave me money for the petrol, and said to buy you a lunch.'

'But not a pony?' Charlie laughed. Then he said, 'Sorry,' because he saw the look on Rowan's face. 'Cheer up. We'll sort it out, one way or another.'

They climbed into the Land-Rover.

'It's a rough old market, this. Anything turns up there, mostly grot. But if you're very lucky, you can get a bargain.'

'Was Fedora a bargain?'

'I think so. Especially if she has a nice foal. When she's had it I want her to go back

81

to racing. She was really good in her day.'

Rowan, hearing the optimism in his voice, wished desperately that she could have a pony, join this fascinating world. If they got Swallow back, would she be able to persuade her father to come to an agreement with Mr Hawes that she might ride him? Perhaps it was in her favour that her father, having been swindled, now wanted the pony back. Her father wasn't very understanding. He would let her have any amount of money if it was for things like school trips, the best trainers or her own computer, but he seemed to think the horse world was unladylike and rough. Babar in her old anorak and gumboots hadn't impressed him. He ought to see Josephine, so elegant and beautiful, riding her tall bay . . . Rowan went into a dream of her father falling for Josephine (only slightly, not enough to leave his wife) and taking her, Rowan, up to High Hawes every evening so that Josephine could give her riding lessons. Then he would buy a trailer and take her to horse shows so that he could watch Josephine compete—

'Damnation,' Charlie said suddenly.

'What's the matter?'

'Our electrics are on the blink.' A red light

was flashing on the dashboard. 'I'll have to pull in and find out what's wrong. Sorry about this.'

It took ages. The fan belt was broken. Charlie said there was a spare somewhere amongst the junk in the back. When he found it, the spanner didn't fit . . . He sweated and swore, attacking the unco-operative bolts. Rowan glanced at her watch. It was gone twelve o'clock and she knew the sale started at ten.

'Hell, I'm sorry,' Charlie said, as he climbed back into the driving seat. 'But we can still trace him, if he went through the ring.'

He zoomed down onto the motorway and drove as fast as the old machine could manage. Rowan, bitterly disappointed, told herself they were on a wild-goose chase anyway but, by the time they turned off and made for the small town where the sale was being held, she was in a bad state of nervous excitement. She had to force herself to keep cool, and not embarrass poor Charlie with her daftness. She bit her tongue to stop it wagging, and got down in the market yard without saying a word.

Charlie seemed to know a lot of people, nodding good-days as he threaded his way through the crowd. In the ring a cow was being sold, the auctioneer chanting on his rostrum in unintelligible fashion, and pens of heifers were waiting to go through the ring. All the horses in sight were tied up to railings or being loaded into lorries, obviously having taken their turn and been sold. Some of the lorries were already driving away – Rowan looked around desperately, aching for a sight of that eager head and the pricked ears, listening for that bellowing whinny.

'We'll go in the office and ask for a look at the books,' Charlie said. 'Norm knows us – he'll know if the pony was here.'

Having a dealer for a father made the task considerably easier. Norm in the office was sympathetic.

'Dark bay fourteen hand gelding? There was a clapped-out twenty-year-old . . . six, you say? Perky beast? Yes, there was one. Looked like a Welshman, very pretty. Not very well-behaved.'

'Was it sold?'

'Yes. Five hundred quid. Its manners put them off.'

'Who to?'

'A Miss Laura Griffiths. She runs a riding school out Arminster way. We know her.'

'Did she pay cash?'

'Aye. It's gone through. Fellow collected it in the office here.'

'The pony's stolen.'

'Bit late to tell us that, Charlie. You should have got here earlier.'

'Yeah. We broke down.'

'You'd better go and see Miss Griffiths about it, Charlie.' Norm looked worried. 'We sold it in good faith. Don't want any trouble.'

'No, it's not your fault.'

Charlie sighed and gave Rowan a wry look. 'Sorry, I've messed it up good and proper. We'll go and see if we can find this woman. You got her address, Norm?'

Norm scribbled it down on the back of an envelope. 'She's probably still around. Pale blue trailer, blue Land-Rover with a white stripe on the side. Go and look in the parking.'

'What's she look like?'

'Young. Early twenties. Pale. Frizzled blonde hair. Worried-looking.'

'OK.'

They left the office and Charlie started to make his way towards the back of the yard where the lorries and trailers were parked.

'At least we've traced him. I doubt if we'll

get him back though. We haven't really got right on our side, have we?'

Rowan managed to choke back her tears. If only they'd been in time! Ken Harvey would have handed him over once he was challenged, she was sure. They would only have had to tell Norm the pony was stolen, and he wouldn't have put it through the ring. She followed Charlie nervously, trying to picture Miss Laura Griffiths. Was she a gentle, loving soul, or a harpy? Worried-looking. What was she worried about? She would have plenty when she found she had bought a stolen pony.

'There's her trailer,' Charlie said suddenly.

It stood between two cattle-floats, apparently deserted. It was rather a broken-down looking combination. On the door of the Land-Rover was written Half Moon Riding Stables.

'Let's have a look.'

Charlie went round to the trailer, opened the groom's door and laughed. 'Here's your chap!'

The eager, familiar face stared out from the gloom and gave a throaty, welcoming nicker. Rowan climbed in and flung her arms round his neck.

'Oh, you darling!' By a terrific feat of self-control she did not burst into tears. She was telling herself at least he was found: if she tried hard enough she knew where he was to buy him back. If she saved all her money, and went out to work (what? where?) and cajoled her father . . . it was all possible. While she had her nose buried in Swallow's thick mane, Miss Laura Griffiths arrived, holding a hot dog to her face and looked understandably surprised.

'Hey—'

Rowan left the explaining to Charlie. She knew Charlie wasn't going to pretend that they legitimately owned the pony; he explained the situation as it was.

'We were going to take it back off this Harvey guy before he got into the sale ring, but as it turned out—' Charlie shrugged.

The undeniably pale Laura Griffiths turned a shade paler at the news and looked horrified.

'I can't be that unlucky! I can't lose my five hundred quid – I'm nearly down the drain as it is! I'm desperate for a pony this size and this market was my only chance. I know most of them are bad 'uns, but I thought this one might turn out OK if he got enough work to stop his nonsense. Which he'll get at my place. I was actually thinking I might have got a bargain. I might have known!'

She looked as if she, like Rowan, could easily burst into tears. Charlie looked worried, surrounded by hysterical females. He gave Rowan a rather frantic look and she, understanding, said hastily, 'It's all right. We're not going to take him back!'

As she spoke these desperate words it was all she could do not to wail aloud. They had missed their chance because of the wretched breakdown and there was no mending the situation.

'He's not ours to take back. Honestly. We know he's not gone to the meat man, that he's going to a good home. That's all that matters,' she lied.

'Except I've bought a stolen animal!'

'In good faith,' Charlie said. 'You can't get into trouble.'

'If the real owners turn up, they can claim him back.'

'Well, if they were going to turn up, I reckon they'd have done so by now. They've had their chance.'

'If they do, you needn't give them my name and address?' Miss Griffiths appealed bleakly.

Charlie shrugged. 'Only if they agreed to buy him back, then we might,' he said.

'I could stand that. But I can't stand losing five hundred quid – no way. Please don't let me in for that!'

'No. Promise. We've all done our best.'

He was obviously anxious to depart, Rowan could see. She took the address of the riding school, went and gave Swallow a final hug and a kiss, and then followed Charlie back to the Land-Rover. She didn't cry, but it took all her resolution not to. They drove away in silence.

About five miles later Charlie said, 'Hell, I'm really sorry about that.'

And the episode of Swallow was over.

CHAPTER SIX

'It's a really daft thing – we've got twenty-five horses in our yard and Rowan wants to learn to ride and we haven't anything suitable to put her on.'

Charlie, having a bad conscience and wanting to comfort Rowan on the way home, had rashly promised that between them, up at High Hawes, they would teach her to ride. Having announced this at the supper table he was met with, 'Who on?'

Hugh jeered, 'Fedora will do. She can hardly put one leg in front of the other.'

'Ha, ha. If you'd taught Cascade manners by now, which any half-decent rider would have done, we could use him.'

'If I had a decent pony instead of Birdie, I could teach her,' Lizzie said.

'She'd do best to ask Babar,' Joan Hawes

90

said. 'You all laugh at her pony, but at least it's safe.'

'We're a dealing yard, not a riding school,' Fred pointed out.

'Yes, well, with two children having left school and wanting to stay at home, I think setting up a riding school department might make us a bit of money.'

The whole family stared at their mother, who was not given to making pronouncements on life-style. Even Fred looked up sharply from his salt beef and dumplings.

Joan went on, 'To diversify is very sensible. We deal chiefly in hunters, and hunting is becoming more threatened every year. If it's not saboteurs, it's local councils or meddling politicians. What will happen to us, Fred, if hunting is banned?'

'God forbid!'

'You should be facing facts, not sticking your head in the sand. Nearly every day the phone rings with some mother asking whether her daughter could come up here for riding lessons, or if not, where could she go? There's absolutely nothing round here. And I just turn away all this good business, because you have Josephine and Charlie schooling hunters all day, instead of teaching little girls.'

The whole family looked at her aghast.

'Teaching little girls!' Charlie's jaw dropped.

'You offered to teach Rowan, I thought.'

'Only Rowan! And only because I owe it to her, making such a boob of getting that pony back.'

'There are dozens of Rowans wanting to be taught. Josephine could make a fortune teaching, with the name she's made for herself at shows.'

Josephine went a shade paler than normal.

'Teaching *beginners*?'

'There's a demand. I'm only stating what's completely obvious. You needn't all look as if I've gone round the bend, for Heaven's sake. It's exactly what Charlie just said – twenty-five horses and not one safe for a beginner. Madness.'

Everyone went on eating, silent, digesting. Lizzie exchanged a glance with Hugh and Hugh raised his eyebrows, but kept his head down. When their mother said something, it was always important. She never wasted words. Her expression was not indignant or heated. Just calm, as ever. Hugh had never wondered about his mother, taking her completely for granted, as one did, but now he wondered a bit, that she never complained or seemed discontented. Rowan's mother, for example, had a cleaning lady for a house that was never dirtied, and did absolutely nothing all day as far as he could see. His mother washed and cleaned and cooked and made clothes and never got hurried or more than mildly cross, and was always there to talk to if you wanted. Not that he did, often, because there wasn't anything to get worried about really. Of course, if the bottom dropped out of their business, there might be. Rowan said she couldn't ever speak to either of her parents about anything that mattered, because they just didn't understand. Hugh had taken it for granted that his mother understood.

'You're suggesting we run a riding school?' Fred asked.

'You're always saying Josephine's entry fees cost a fortune. She might earn them, if just in the evenings, after school. A class of six, say, three times a week . . . people keep asking. Start with Rowan.'

'What on?'

'Exactly. Back to square one.'

No more was said at the time, but Joan's words were not forgotten. Josephine supposed she ought to see about passing her British Horse Society teachers' thing – even if she never did actually get round to teaching, it might come in useful if she ever left home and wanted a job; Fred told himself he would look round for a few decent children's ponies, and Lizzie and Hugh decided they would give Rowan a lesson on Cascade and see what happened.

'As long as we don't let go of him—'

'Couldn't we put him on the lunge?'

'He might buck.'

'Well, she's got to learn to fall off. It's all part of it.'

'Not in her first lesson.'

They announced the news to Rowan, that she was to come up for her first ride.

'Who's going to teach me?' Her eyes glowed, thinking Charlie.

'We are,' said Hugh. 'Lizzie and me.'

Rowan went quiet. Hugh was so bossy, a real budding MCP. But Lizzie, who was (Rowan knew) afraid of Birdie, would know how she felt. If she was there it would be all right.

'We'll lend you a hat and things.' Lizzie guessed that Mrs Watkins was likely to rush out and buy a black showing jacket and £100 jods if she heard the news. 'You might hate it, you never know.'

Rowan could not believe that. 'Tonight?'

'Tonight? Oh well, why not?' Hugh's enthusiasm was dying off quite quickly.

After school, before Rowan came, he rode Cascade out and tried to make him tired, but Cascade was so fit he didn't get tired, only excited, which Hugh realized (too late) was a mistake. He tried to cool him down, riding him round the manège but it was so *boring*.

'I'm not cut out to be a teacher,' he said to Lizzie.

'Bad luck,' she said. 'She's here.'

Mr Watkins had brought her up in the car. Lizzie and Hugh were terrified he was going to stay and watch. The Watkins had insisted on paying for the lesson, which was very worrying. If Cascade bucked her off, Hugh decided, they would give the money back.

But, thank goodness, Mr Watkins drove away, and Rowan came out to the manège with Lizzie, fastening up her borrowed helmet.

'First, you must learn to mount,' Lizzie said. 'Hugh will demonstrate.'

Hugh demonstrated. Then he got off and

showed how he could vault on, and after two vaults, he showed Rowan how he could run up from behind and jump up astride Cascade's rump.

'If I took the saddle off, I'd land in the right place,' he said. 'Like a cowboy robbing a bank.'

'Look,' Lizzie said. 'This is a riding lesson, to learn to do it properly. Not a circus audition.'

'He's brilliant at gymkhana,' said Hugh. He wanted to add, So am I, but thought it was rather too boastful, so said instead, 'We're in the Prince Philip team.'

'What's the Prince Philip team?'

'The mounted games team, for the Pony Club. You know, the finalists do it on television. We've been in the final, me and Cascade.'

'Oh, do shut up, Hugh,' Lizzie said. 'You didn't win. This is supposed to be a riding lesson. Come and hold Cascade and I'll show Rowan how to mount.'

Rowan managed to get on the proper way and Lizzie showed her how to hold the reins. After that Lizzie and Hugh supposed you just walked round. They couldn't think of anything else, except keep your heels down, elbows in and squeeze a sponge with your hands. That only took a minute and there still were fifty minutes to go. Pressing with her heels to move on was quite unnecessary, as Cascade was champing to go faster.

'He feels very joggy,' Rowan said rather anxiously.

'He'll settle down when he realizes it's not jumping,' Lizzie said.

Cascade had never walked round the manège without being asked to do anything. He got nervous, stopping and starting, wondering at the strange feel in his saddle. Nobody but Hugh had ridden him for two years.

'He might go better on the lunge,' Hugh decided. 'He knows what's wanted, on the lunge.'

Lizzie was undecided, but Hugh went off to the tack room and came back with the long lunging rein and head-collar. He put it on and said to Lizzie, 'You can do it.'

The idea was that the pony went round Lizzie in large circles, on the end of the rein, obeying her voice, while Rowan got the feel of things. Hugh sat on the fence looking bored, thinking how quite extraordinary it was that a person couldn't ride. What was so difficult about it? He just couldn't see. Yet Rowan couldn't even walk without lurching about and looking terrified.

'Relax,' Lizzie said.

Clever idea, Hugh thought. Perhaps Lizzie was a born teacher and would make the Hawes fortune. People who can, do; people who couldn't, taught; he remembered the saying. It was true that some of the best riding teachers he knew of (he had never had a lesson, as such, only been shouted at by his father) had never been seen on a horse themselves.

Suddenly there was a loud scream and Rowan came flying through the air in his direction, to land on the edge of the manège with a terrific flump. She hit her head on the wooden fence with a crack that shook the whole rail and lay still. Hugh felt his jaw drop open with amazement. Lizzie dropped the rein and ran towards Rowan, and Cascade took to his heels and went tearing round the manège bucking and fly-kicking.

'Catch your stupid pony!' Lizzie screamed at him.

'What happened?' Hugh hadn't taken it in at all.

'He let out an enormous buck. He's really

stupid! Just like his owner!' She was jibbering with fury.

Hugh looked at Rowan, feeling a bit sick. Lizzie dropped down beside her. Rowan lay face down with her nose in the peat and appeared to be quite unconscious.

'What shall we do?'

'She'll come round in a minute. We don't want Mum and Dad to know, for goodness sake! Rowan!' Lizzie hissed in Rowan's ear.

'Is she breathing?' Hugh asked. 'You're supposed to put a mirror up to their nostrils and it mists over if they're still alive.'

'Oh, do shut up, if you can't say anything more intelligent! She's saying something. Her lips are moving. She's coming round. Rowan!'

Lizzie gave Rowan a little shake and moved her head to the side.

'You shouldn't move her in case she's broken her neck.'

'*Shut up!* Rowan, can you hear me?'

Rowan groaned and her eyes opened.

'Hooray,' said Hugh. 'It's nothing.' But he knew the feeling.

'Rowan! It's me, Lizzie. Can you see me? Are you all right?'

Hugh left them to it and went to catch

Cascade, who was now standing by the gate, obviously not wanting to be a riding school pony. He looked anxiously at Hugh, aware of his disobedience. But Hugh was on his side. He took off the lunging rein and said, 'It's all right, mate.' They went back to the stable yard and Hugh put Cascade away and hung up the tack. There was no-one around save Charlie who was starting evening feeds.

'That was a very short lesson,' Charlie said.

Hugh hesitated. He looked out of the back window of the feed room and saw that Rowan was still lying down, although she seemed to be talking.

'He bucked her off,' Hugh said.

'Jeez, you're hopeless,' Charlie said. 'Can't you control that pony at all?'

'She got knocked out.'

Charlie, shocked, dropped the feedbin lid. 'You idiots!'

He hurried out to the school and Rowan was able to focus her blurred vision on lovely Charlie, his gypsy eyes staring with great concern into her own. After ascertaining that there was nothing seriously wrong, Charlie picked her up and carried her back to the tack room. Rowan, in Charlie's arms, felt it was worth being bucked off for. She felt fuzzy but secure, initiated into this glorious life. He laid her tenderly in the dog-hairy armchair beneath the rows of saddles and said, 'I'll get Mum to ring yours, and she can take you to the surgery. Concussion can be dangerous.'

With one breath, Rowan, Lizzie and Hugh exclaimed, 'No!'

'I'm not concussed,' Rowan said quickly. 'Honestly.'

'Don't tell them,' Hugh said crossly. 'It'll spoil everything.'

'We'll get into awful trouble,' Lizzie said.

'You mustn't!' Rowan said. 'You know what my parents are like! They'll fuss terribly, and not let me come here any more.'

Charlie frowned, knowing they were right.

'Nobody saw. I'll be quite all right in ten minutes,' Rowan said. 'Honestly.'

The threat of her parents knowing terrified her. Her father would kick up a terrible furore and talk about suing. And they would never, ever let me have a riding lesson again.

Charlie, thank goodness, realized the danger.

'No, well. I can see what you mean.'

But he was worried by being in collusion,

responsible enough to know the seriousness of it.

'You wouldn't have known if I hadn't told you,' Hugh very reasonably pointed out. 'Go back to feeding and pretend you don't know anything. You'll spoil everything if you tell.'

'Please!' Rowan said. 'I'm fine, really,' she lied.

'OK.' He was dubious, but departed.

'Thank goodness for that!' Lizzie said. 'I'll make you a cup of tea, Rowan. That's good for shock.'

There was a kettle and tea things in the tack room and she made the tea and Rowan sat in the armchair convincing herself that she felt all right. She tried standing up, but had to hastily sit down again, as the room tipped from side to side as if they were at sea. Her head ached hideously.

'You're sort of green,' Hugh said, not very helpfully.

'She'll be all right in half an hour,' Lizzie snapped.

'I feel a bit sick,' Rowan admitted.

'Don't worry,' said Lizzie. 'We've all done it. Charlie broke a vertebra when he was fourteen and Hugh was out for four hours once.'

'Five,' Hugh said.

'Don't swank.'

'Lucky it was right at the beginning of the lesson,' Hugh said. 'You've still got three-quarters of an hour to get better. Is your father coming back for you?'

'I told him not to, but he said he would.'

By the time the hour was up Rowan could walk in a straight line, although she felt terrible. They waited in an anxious row as Mr Watkins drove into the yard. Luckily it was going dusk and he didn't notice Rowan's pallor.

'How was it?' He was in a good mood for once. 'Enjoy yourself?'

'Yes, it was great.' Rowan grinned hugely.

'So how much do I owe you young people?' He groped around and pulled out his wallet.

'Oh no, really, we don't want any money,' Lizzie said hurriedly.

'Come. I insist. She'll want to come again, won't she? We must have it on a business-like footing.'

He insisted on giving Lizzie £10. She thought it was a fortune, even if the lesson had been phenomenally successful. She blushed scarlet and tried to refuse it but Mr Watkins would have none of it.

'A one to one lesson – that's the going rate, I'm sure. Well done, all of you. Come along, Rowan.'

Rowan staggered to the car and got in and he whisked her away out of the yard, leaving Lizzie and Hugh staring in horror at the £10 note.

'She'll never come again! Fancy getting paid that for nearly killing her!'

They went and told Charlie and he laughed and said he would take care of it for them.

Meanwhile Rowan went home and was sick in the bathroom, but came down and talked enthusiastically about how she had enjoyed her lesson. It took an enormous effort. Her mother said she looked pale. 'It must be the excitement.'

'What are we going to do?' On the school bus the next morning, Rowan was still a green colour and had to keep her eyes shut. 'I was so good at saying how much I enjoyed it my father says he'll bring me up again next week, and my mother's going to buy me jods and everything. She's got friendly with Mrs Prebble, and now she thinks it's all a wonderful

104

idea.' She sighed deeply, and had to admit: 'I can't face riding Cascade again. I'll be terrified. I'm useless.'

'No. It's him that's useless. We wouldn't dream of putting you back on him.'

'What'll we do then?'

'We can just pretend you have a lesson, and take the money,' Hugh said. Was he serious? He was grinning.

'If you weren't so useless, the pony would have some manners,' Lizzie shouted at him.

Rowan's head ached abominably and the landscape swam in green arcs beyond the window. At school she kept her head down in class and hid from the teachers, and was sick once more in the lavatory at break time. She felt rather desperate. The effort at home in the evening, being bright, exhausted her. Her mother kept giving her strange looks. 'Are you sure you feel all right, dear? There's flu about, I hear. You're dreadfully pale.'

'I'm fine!' Big, bright smile. Knife stabs in the cranium.

But as the week went on she gradually recovered. Only the thought of the next lesson made her feel ill again. Was she really such a wimp? But both Lizzie and Hugh said it was quite normal to be put off by such a happening.

Unfortunately Hugh let out what had happened in front of his mother, and Joan Hawes came out to find Rowan. She gave her a lecture.

'If that ever happens again, don't take any notice of my stupid children, but tell your mother and go to the doctor. Concussion can be very serious and needs rest to cure it. I'm very angry with Hugh and Lizzie.'

'I'm quite all right now, honestly!'

'Well, you look it, I must admit. But remember what I've said. You are all old enough to act responsibly. It was really stupid to put a beginner on Cascade. I don't know what to suggest you ride – but certainly not that one again.'

It was Charlie who came up with the solution. 'You must go and see Babar,' he said to Lizzie, 'And get her to ride up here on Diamond. And Rowan can have her lesson on Diamond and you can give Babar the money. She'll be terribly pleased.'

'Can't we keep any of it?' Hugh asked.

'No.'

'But we're the *agents*. Agents always keep at least ten per cent.'

'You didn't do anything at all, except vault on Cascade just to show off,' Lizzie said. 'So I don't see why you should even think of having any of it.'

Mr Watkins' eager gifts of £10 notes had set them all thinking what an easy way it was to make money. 'Mum's right, really. We could teach children if we had some decent ponies,' Lizzie said. 'At least, I could. Hugh was useless.'

'You could teach the beginners,' Hugh said. 'I could take them on when they were more advanced. Jumping.'

'Huh!'

Shrimp came out with 'Horse and Hound' and showed them a large coloured photograph of a pony at a show covered in rosettes and herself astride, gazing haughtily at the camera.

'Yuk,' said Hugh.

'I'm going to pin it up in the tack room,' Shrimp said. 'It's rather nice.'

'Don't put it near my tack. I might vomit.'

'Your tack's so filthy a bit of sick on it wouldn't make any difference.'

They were used to seeing Shrimp picked up by smart horse-boxes or expensive cars at weekends to be whisked away to big shows, carrying her bag of immaculate gear. When she was younger (six) her mother had gone with her, but now she was such a professional she went on her own, the rich showing family she rode for treating her like one of their own. Lizzie and Hugh wondered why she didn't die of boredom – 'You don't even have to jump!' – but in their hearts they knew that she was worth her weight in gold to the pony owners, showing their – often difficult – ponies with a rare expertise.

'Mum says you're going to give lessons. I've come to watch.'

'Jeer, I suppose?'

Shrimp grinned. She was amazingly composed for a nine-year-old – all that show-biz, Lizzie supposed. 'Do you want to do it, as you know everything?'

'No fear. Only watch.'

But Lizzie knew it would be all right with the phlegmatic Diamond. Babar was utterly reliable. She arrived at the right time and Rowan got on Diamond without any fear and they all trailed out to the manège. Babar turned out to be an excellent teacher, much better than Lizzie, and in the end Lizzie let her take over and sat on the fence with Shrimp. (Hugh had lost interest now that

Cascade wasn't involved and nobody would let him share in the £10.) Babar got Rowan trotting and Diamond even lurched into a few canter steps without Rowan coming adrift. Rowan found her confidence, and thoroughly enjoyed herself. She was confident that the stolid Diamond would play no tricks, and his long flopping ears ahead of her flitched agreeably like a seaside donkey's. She felt none of the tremors of alarm that had exuded from Cascade at the feel of her insecurity. Riding was suddenly full of fun and hope, and her past week of depression and disappointment was forgotten.

'What a nag!' Shrimp whispered to Lizzie. 'I wouldn't be seen dead on it.'

'He does the job,' Lizzie said sharply. It was a long time since she had felt the enjoyment in riding that she now saw Rowan revealing. Why did she have to suffer Birdie with all her traumas, when an old steady like Diamond – well, prettier – was all her unadventurous heart desired? Perhaps Charlie could persuade their father to sell Birdie to the Prebbles. Smartypants Matty was welcome to her.

'You're a much better teacher than me,' she said to Babar, when they had finished. 'You might as well teach Rowan and let Mr Watkins know it's you.'

She looked so disappointed that Babar said kindly, 'We can still come up here and use your school. Mr Watkins needn't know anything different.'

'And share the money,' Rowan said. 'Would that be fair?'

'Babar does everything. She should have more than half,' Lizzie said.

'I don't want the money. I like doing it,' Babar said.

'We could save the money, to buy Rowan her own pony!' Lizzie said.

'Buy Swallow back!'

'What a good idea! We'll save it!'

Now Lizzie wished she could have it after all, to save to buy herself a pony. It was her idea and she had wasted it on Rowan, speaking without thinking. Then, seeing Rowan's shining face, she was ashamed.

'When you've learned to ride a bit,' she said, 'You could go over to that riding stable that bought Swallow, and have a lesson on him.'

'Oh, what a brilliant idea!'

'He's probably settled down now, with plenty of work, and he'd be much easier.'

Rowan was thrilled with these amazing ideas. Babar departed on Diamond, and Rowan and Lizzie trailed into the tack room where Rowan took her hat off and sat down in the armchair. She felt a bit feeble. Charlie came in to fetch a head-collar.

'I'm going to bring Fedora in. She looks off-colour.'

'She's turned pink?' Shrimp said.

Charlie gave her a cold look. 'She's not eating. She's tucked up.'

'When is her foal due?' Rowan asked.

'Six weeks yet.'

Charlie looked worried. He went out and Shrimp said, 'Why is he so potty on that terrible old mare?'

'Because she's his own,' Lizzie said. 'Not Dad's. And he remembers her when she looked wonderful, racing at Newbury. And he thinks she can be like that again. And the foal – the foal might be marvellous.'

'I think he's mad.' Shrimp departed with a toss of her head.

'Isn't she horrible?' Lizzie said to Rowan.

'She's absolutely heartless. So cocky. We all hate her.'

Perhaps, Rowan thought, there was something to be said for being an only.

That night, Fred Hawes had his first heart attack.

CHAPTER SEVEN

'What do you mean, a heart attack?' Mrs Watkins asked. 'How bad? Is he in hospital?'

'They took him there. Then he came home again. No, it's not bad but he's got to rest. He passed out and went peculiar.'

'Well, I expect he'll be all right. They give you tablets for things like that these days.'

'It's very hard for him to rest,' Rowan pointed out. 'He goes all over the place, buying horses.'

'That boy of his will have to do it.'

Rowan, immersed in life at High Hawes, knew it wasn't as easy as that. Charlie and Josephine worked full-time looking after and tuning the horses their father brought home. When buyers came, they had to show them off. Fred Hawes hadn't sat on a horse since he was six, but he had an eye for a horse second to none, and acquired bargains which less astute dealers missed. Nobody could do his job. Rowan had heard her friends muttering between themselves about what would happen if their father had to lay up. Gloom had noticeably descended.

But Rowan had more immediate things on her mind.

'Charlie's mare is due to foal any minute now. He says I can go and watch, but it'll most likely be in the night.'

'Well, if it's in the night, I'm afraid not.'

'It would only be half an hour or so!'

'Absolutely not. You've your school work to think of. You wouldn't sleep a wink, all the excitement.'

Rowan reported back at High Hawes. 'I've never seen anything born! Not even a kitten.'

'Oh, it's all bloody and yukky. You haven't missed anything,' said Hugh. 'Great judders and slime.'

'I bet you were slimy when you came out,' Shrimp said.

'It's wonderful,' Charlie said. 'You ought to see it.'

'I'm going to, Charlie. Promise! Promise you'll wake me!' Shrimp badgered.

'You could get out of bed and come up, Rowan,' Hugh suggested. 'They wouldn't hear you, would they?'

'How would I know?'

'We could send a signal. Light a bonfire, like the Armada.'

'I could turn on the school floodlight. You'd see that,' Charlie suggested.

'I can see that from my bed!'

'Well, then. She'll warn us, after all. I'll know roughly. If it's imminent, I'll switch on the light. Even if you miss it – it's usually very quick – at least you'll see the foal newborn.'

Rowan could tell Charlie was quite excited at the prospect. Fedora was heavy and bad-tempered and due any day. It was better thinking about the new life than thinking about Fred, and the problems with the yard. In spite of their all agreeing that their mother's idea about having a teaching sideline and a business in children's ponies was a good one, no-one had done anything about it. Babar had gone on teaching Rowan on Diamond, and Rowan was pronounced to be 'quite competent'. 'You need something better than Diamond, but you're not ready yet for Cascade or Birdie,' was the general opinion.

Rowan didn't think she would ever be ready for Cascade or Birdie. She hadn't forgotten that they had planned to go over to the riding stable that had bought Swallow, but nobody had mentioned it again. She wanted to go terribly but she didn't want to go on her own.

'Will you come with me?' she asked Lizzie. 'We could use the money in the pot.' This was the money Mr Watkins insisted on paying for her lessons, which was now something of an embarrassment. They kept it in an instant-coffee jar hidden behind a box of wormers.

Lizzie looked doubtful. 'I don't really *want* to. It's such a long way, just for a ride. Why don't you ask Babar?'

Rowan asked Babar. Babar said yes, why not? She had never ridden anything but Diamond.

'We could go on Saturday morning. There's a bus. We don't want a lesson, like, just a hack.'

'Yes, I'll arrange it! I'll ring them up. I'll say a hack. And I'll ask for Swallow!'

'Tell 'um how you ride, like – not very experienced.'

'Yes, I'll say that. But you're good.'

'I'm only good on Diamond. I dunno what another's like, do I?'

Her parents agreed to Rowan's request, thinking it could do no harm to humour her this once, and Rowan duly rang to book the ride. The girl called Laura Griffiths sounded weary and hesitated when Rowan asked for Swallow. 'I suppose that'll be all right,' she said.

Rowan wasn't encouraged, but soon forgot about it in her excitement. She told Lizzie and Lizzie said, 'He'll probably buck you off, like Cascade.'

Hugh said, 'Fedora's going to go splat tonight, Charlie says.'

'You are *foul*,' Lizzie said to him.

'I'm going to stay up all night,' Shrimp said. 'Charlie's going to, aren't you, Charlie?'

'Probably. I'll see, later.'

It was a fine, soft evening smelling of summer and May blossom. The hedges up from the village were untrimmed and spilled their white flowers like confetti across the bumpy tarmac. The fields were lush with spring grass and the buttercups that made Fred Hawes swear, and in the woods above the farm the rooks homed in on their untidy nests with a great squawking and flapping against the cloudless sky. Rowan longed to ride through the woods up onto the downs with Lizzie and Hugh, but it was impossible to borrow Diamond and leave Babar behind. She longed for her own pony. Her parents kept saying, 'Well, later, we'll think about it.'

Rowan went out across the yard to visit Fedora, who was in her loose-box round the back – 'Keep that ugly mare out of my sale yard,' Fred had ordered. But Rowan didn't think Fedora was ugly any more, with her gaunt flanks filled out and the scars faded from her legs. Her summer coat gleamed although she was never groomed, a rich, bright chestnut, and her once-despondent eyes were now bright and – it must be said – irritable. She switched her fine red tail nervously at Rowan's approach. One had to handle her with care. Rowan only looked, out of range. Drips of milk were running down her back legs, and a sheen of sweat had broken out over her shoulders.

'Oh, come on, have it now,' Rowan urged her. 'Don't wait till midnight!'

Charlie was restless too, and came to have a look.

'She won't be long.'

'I must see it!'

'Ask your Mum to let you stay. Ring her up.'

'Shall I?'

'It's worth a try.'

'Until ten o'clock,' her mother said, as a great concession. 'Then, if nothing's happening, you must come straight home.'

'She'll be later than that. They like the dark,' Charlie said. 'But you never know.'

'What do you want, a colt or a filly?'

'I don't care. Just a good one. It should be – her owner knew what he was doing. He bred some good horses in his day. He's bound to have sent her to a good stallion.'

But by ten o'clock, Fedora had settled down and was munching her hay. Rowan, deeply disappointed, ran home down the hill and went to bed. She slept heavily, her window open.

Something woke her. The house was silent and it was pitch dark, save for one bright light distant across the fields. Rowan lay looking at the light. It wasn't usually there. Then she remembered – the signal! She slipped out of bed and ran to the window. The school light – she could see clearly now where it came from. Fedora was having her foal!

Rowan dragged a jersey over her pyjamas, thrust her feet into her sandals and slipped downstairs. It didn't matter if her parents woke

– she would be away before they realized. But she was neat and silent and out of the house without disturbing anybody, dragging her bike out of the shed and hopping onto the pedals. Her excitement fired her up the hill. She skidded into the yard, breathless, dropped the bike and ran.

There was a light on in Fedora's box. Shrimp was hanging over the door, presumably excluded by Charlie.

'Rowan – good! I remembered the light! She's started, but Charlie won't let me in.'

Rowan looked over the door and saw that the mare was lying down. She was grunting and threshing her legs about, and Charlie sat in the straw by her head, talking softly to her. He looked up and saw Rowan and grinned. 'Well done!'

'How long will she be?'

'No time at all, if we're lucky.'

Rowan could tell he was really excited. She felt nervous and a bit queer. Something was happening, she could see, and now she was here she didn't want to look.

'It's got white socks!' Shrimp squeaked.

'God Almighty!' Charlie breathed.

Rowan didn't understand.

'It's got a white nose!' Shrimp shouted. 'Charlie, it's white!'

Rowan forced herself to look and saw a most extraordinary thing. The foal appeared before her very eyes, as if conjured, diving out into the fresh straw with its front legs pointing forward and its little head laid on its paws like a dog. It was tiny and a most remarkable colour: white with large chestnut patches. A circus horse.

'I don't believe it!'

Rowan saw that Charlie was pole-axed. He looked thunderous. Shrimp was laughing.

'What a marvellous, marvellous foal!'

'It's a travesty – a freak! It's rubbish! I don't believe it!'

Rowan could see that Charlie was close to tears with disappointment. Ignorant as she was, even she could see that this was a very strange produce from a large chestnut thoroughbred. Fedora groaned with relief and turned her elegant neck to see what lay in the straw behind her. She stretched out her neck as if to lick it, but instead she laid back her ears and bit it. A startled squeak of pain came from the little foal.

'Yeah, that's just how I feel, old girl. We don't want it, do we?'

'Charlie!' Shrimp squeaked. 'You can't say that!'

'She's going to reject it.'

The foal was already making great efforts to get to its feet. It scrabbled and swayed on its haunches, thrusting to get up. Half up, it was then knocked backwards by an angry Fedora with another thrust of her bared teeth. She started to get up, scraping up the straw. Charlie stood watching. Undaunted, the foal was struggling helplessly to get its legs back underneath it. Charlie made no effort to help it. He just stood with his hands in his pockets.

'Charlie!' Shrimp cried, 'You must do something! She'll hurt it!'

'She'll kill it. Best thing,' Charlie said.

He turned away and came to the door and unshot the bolt. Although he was framed against the light, Rowan thought there were tears in his eyes. He came out and shut the door behind him.

Shrimp screamed at him, 'Charlie! You can't!'

But Charlie was already walking back to the house. Over his shoulder he muttered, 'I'll come back in a bit, clear her up.' He disappeared round the corner of the barn.

Shrimp burst into loud blubbing tears and unbolted the stable door.

'You'll help me, won't you?' she sobbed to Rowan. 'He's *beastly*! He can't—'

Rowan was appalled. Like Shrimp, she couldn't possibly stand by and watch the little defenceless foal being bullied. Fedora's ears were flat back and she was trembling and sweating, half up, her forelegs out in front of her.

'Go and fetch a head-rope – quick!' Shrimp screamed at Rowan.

Rowan fled. Charlie had unlocked the tack-room door and the light was on. She pulled down a rope and sprinted back to the loose-box. Fedora was wearing a head-collar. Rowan flung the rope at Shrimp over the door and saw Shrimp clip it onto the head-collar just before Fedora, with an angry plunge, got to her feet. Shrimp was tiny at the head of the big, disturbed mare. Rowan, terrified, knew she had to go into the box to help. She unbolted the door and went in. Shrimp just managed to slip the head-rope through the ring-bolt on the wall, but Fedora flung round and it flew out of Shrimp's hand.

'Help me! Hang on!' Shrimp bellowed.

Rowan jumped forward and grabbed the rope and jerked on it with all her strength as Fedora turned and made a plunge towards the foal. She stopped her, but the mare was much stronger than she was. Shrimp, like an angry wasp, leapt for the end of the rope and threaded it through the ring-bolt again and made a knot. She was so quick and deft that the mare was held before she had a chance to pull away again. Unable to use her teeth, she lashed out with her hindlegs. The foal was lying behind her, right in the line of fire. The first kick missed but the second caught the foal on the shoulder and tore off a long strip of skin. Bright blood sprung across the snow-white coat and the foal let out another pathetic squeak, dropping back into the straw.

Rowan could feel her heart pounding heavily and the tears spurting down her cheeks. They had to drag the foal away, but the mare's heels were lethal. Shrimp was as desperate as she was.

'Go and get a fork, a mucking-out fork!'

The loose-box was a very dangerous place to be. It was big, fortunately, and there was room to pull the foal away if they could brave the awful heels. Shrimp, born into horses, knew things Rowan could not fathom . . . a fork? But Rowan fled to do her bidding. Fedora was making strange noises and rolling her eyes. Rowan went in with the fork and gave it to Shrimp. Shrimp grabbed it and brandished it at Fedora. She looked like a little Boadicea, her hair standing on end, her eyes flashing with fury.

'You *beast*! You *horrid, horrid* animal!' And she jabbed the fork into Fedora's flank. 'Get over!' she roared. 'Get over!'

Fedora made one step sideways and lashed out again. But this time she missed the foal. She jerked at her head but – thank heavens, Rowan breathed – the rope and leather head-collar held. If she got free Rowan thought they would all be killed.

'Get the foal, Rowan!' Shrimp screamed at her. 'Pull it away! Quick!'

Without hesitating Rowan sprang forward. There was nothing to get hold of: the little animal was all slimy and wet and had no handles, only the enormous trembling legs flailing feebly. Its little head struggled up and Rowan looked into its bewildered eyes. She grabbed it, one arm round its neck and the other round its hind quarters. As she did so Fedora lashed out again, in spite of the fork, and the hoof whistled past Rowan's head so close that she felt the wind of its passing. Shrimp jabbed Fedora with the fork so hard that she drew blood.

'Quick! Quick!'

Rowan dragged, half-rolled, the foal across the floor, at one point pulling it by the back legs. Shrimp, made strong by her fury, held the mare at bay with determined jabs at her flanks.

'Get it outside!'

Although it was small it was still a very heavy animal. Rowan reached up to push the door open and pulled the foal bodily by its back legs. There was no other way. Out in the yard she fell over, and hadn't the strength to do any more than lie there, beside the foal. She was shaking like a sail head to wind, half with terror, half with her effort. In an instant Shrimp was beside her, kicking the door shut and ramming home the bolt. She then leaned against the door, shaking as much as Rowan.

'The beast!' she sobbed. 'The beastly mare!'

'But it's all right, Shrimp!' Rowan said. Her two years' superiority in age asserted itself as she realized what a state Shrimp was in, worse than herself. 'We've won!' she said. 'The foal's all right.'

With its instinct for survival the foal was once more struggling to get up. The sight of its antics calmed the hysterics. There was still much to be done.

'Glory!' Shrimp breathed. 'It's ours, Rowan! We've got to look after it!'

Shrimp was a girl of action, as she had already proved. She went round the barn to Cascade's box and led him out and let him loose in the field, then came back to Rowan and the foal. Rowan had managed, with her arms round its backside and chest, to get it to stand. The feel of its frailty and yet the urge to struggle and live moved her incredibly. The fact that they had saved its life was almost like having given it birth herself and they were both now imbued with a godlike bliss. It was an extraordinary little animal, a pony foal, with an outsize will to make good. Out of the furious, nearly seventeen-hand thoroughbred . . . 'Why?' Rowan asked. 'What happened?'

'Some pikey pony got loose, I should think, and couldn't believe its luck, finding Fedora in a field somewhere. Poor old Charlie.'

Shrimp giggled. With one on each side

steadying it, the foal was guided round the corner into Cascade's box. Shrimp put the light on and shut the door and the two girls stood looking at it in wonder. It was a skewbald, well marked, with bold patches of dark chestnut over white. Its head was chestnut but with a white blaze, and its front and back legs were white. It stood firmly now, just swaying slightly, and its expression was one of puzzlement and anxiety. Rowan thought: half an hour ago it was inside Fedora. The miracle of birth was hard to take in, even without the panics of this particular one. Rowan felt drained, and not quite all there.

Shrimp, looking underneath it, said, 'It's a colt.' Then, 'It's mine. My own. I shall bring it up by hand.'

'Why, won't Fedora take it eventually?'

'Once they reject a foal, that's it, usually.'

'Do you have to feed it with a bottle?'

'Yes. Every two hours at first. We've done it before, with a thoroughbred. We took turns.' Remembering, she added, 'It was awful.' Her face dropped then, and she looked very white and little. 'I will do it, though.' She looked sternly at Rowan. 'They think I don't like work, don't they? They're always saying it.

They think I'm stupid. I'll show Hugh. He wouldn't do it, I bet.'

'I'll help you,' Rowan said.

'Yes. If you hadn't come . . . it needed two of us, didn't it?' She grinned and put her arms round the foal and kissed it. It pushed its nuzzle at her, looking for its mother. Shrimp started to look worried. 'We need to feed it now. Soon.'

'What, with cow's milk?'

'No. Special stuff. We've got some, some-where.' Shrimp considered. 'Would you go and fetch Charlie? He won't have gone to bed, because he's got to come back and see to Fedora. The foal ought to have Fedora's first milk, because it has special good things in it, to make the foal thrive. He can jolly well get that for us, milk it off. You ask him. He's more likely to do it if you ask him.'

Rowan was nervous of this job. She knew Charlie was upset, and approached the house with trepidation. He would be cross at her interfering and snap her head off. Shrimp wouldn't have been able to do it by herself, it was true. Shrimp . . . she should have been called Spitfire, Rowan thought.

The light was on in the kitchen. Rowan went in, feeling rather shaky. The clock on the wall said two-thirty. Rowan had never been out and about at two-thirty in the morning before. She certainly didn't feel sleepy.

Charlie was sitting at the kitchen table with his head lying on his arms, looking asleep. But he heard Rowan and sat up.

'Shrimp sent me,' Rowan said quickly.

'You should have gone home,' Charlie said angrily.

'She wants you to — to do something . . . when you go out to Fedora.'

Charlie didn't say anything, just sat with his head in his hands.

'We've put the foal in Cascade's box.'

He flung round furiously. 'That's a stupid thing to do! Now what? In a case like that you let nature take over. Nobody wants a runt like that — who's going to rear it? All that work, for rubbish!'

'Shrimp is. We are.'

'You've no idea!'

He was so angry, Rowan was frightened. She stood feeling really miserable, the night that should have been so lovely shattered by his disappointment.

'I'm sorry,' she muttered. 'The way it turned out . . . for you.'

'It was going to be my own, my very own, out of a good mare . . . I was an idiot to make dreams. With horses – dreams hardly ever work out – '

As if she didn't know! Perhaps he recognized this, for he made an obvious effort to pull himself together, and gave her a hint of a smile.

'Sorry. I didn't mean to take it out on you.'

Rowan felt a great surge of passionate love for Charlie and wanted to throw her arms round his neck and comfort him, but the thought gave her a hint of the giggles, and she merely smiled instead, thankful his awful rage had dissipated. He was her hero . . . had he really shed tears? She was pretty sure he had. She was awed.

He got up and shrugged into his jacket.

'If Shrimp – and you – want to rear this foal, it will depend a bit on Father, and Mum. After all, you've got to be at school all day, and sleep at night. You don't know what you're taking on. Father will say, like me, it isn't worth it. I'm warning you. What Mum and Dad decide, will be it. So don't count on it.'

Rowan's heart plummeted. They wouldn't let it die, surely?

'It might be best to shoot it.'

Rowan felt her throat swell as if she had swallowed an apple whole, and didn't dare say anything.

'But for now,' Charlie said, 'we'd better appease Shrimp – she's a nutter.'

Rowan went back with him to Fedora's box, and stood looking over the door while Charlie worked over her. She was still in a very disturbed state, and he was very gentle with her, talking to her softly. He cleaned the box of the mess and put a sweat rug on the mare.

'Shrimp said – she wants the milk, the first milk.' Rowan forced out her instructions.

'The colostrum? OK.'

Charlie now seemed back to his calm self. To milk the mare was a three-person job: one to hold up a front leg to stop her kicking, one to hold the bucket and one to milk. Charlie was agreeable because he thought the mare would be more comfortable and settle down better. But once the milk was in the bucket he left the girls to their own devices. He did not want to set eyes on the foal, and when Fedora was let loose and had stopped sweating and stamping, he went back to bed.

Shrimp hunted for the bottle that was somewhere in the yard's first-aid cupboard.

Together, at three o'clock in the morning, Rowan and Shrimp sat in the straw and gave their funny little foal its first food. After all the excitement, they both felt overwhelmed with pure pleasure and love for the foal, each other, life, and the world. Rowan had never felt so emotional, not even over Swallow.

At four o'clock she left Shrimp curled up in the straw with the foal lying beside her, and set off down the hill for home. The sky was thin with the flush of dawn, pale and grey and soft and smelling of dew and summer. She wanted to drink it in, feeling it too rare and good to miss. Life seemed almost too much to take in; she felt as if she was bursting.

Tomorrow's – today's! – problems could wait.

CHAPTER EIGHT

It was Joan Hawes who saved the life of Fedora's foal. Fred said it should be put down, Charlie agreed, even Josephine said it wasn't worth the trouble of hand-feeding. Lizzie, Hugh and Shrimp staunchly vowed to look after it.

'Take it to school with you, on the bus?' Their father was dismissive. 'Don't be ridiculous.'

Joan, with a sympathetic glance towards the white-faced Shrimp, said calmly, 'I will feed it while they are at school. They can take it in turns at night.'

'Oh, Mum!' Shrimp flung her arms round her mother's neck. 'Rowan will share too, I know she will. Oh, thank-you, thank-you, thank-you!'

'Good, Rowan can do my share,' Hugh said.

'Babar will help, I bet,' said Lizzie.

'But it's mine, remember,' Shrimp shouted. 'It's my foal!'

'Yes,' said her mother. 'I shall certainly remember. It is yours, and you will do all the mucking out and all the looking-after when you are at home.'

'I won't go to any more shows. I shall stay at home all the time.'

'No. You can't let your owners down like that, without warning. You must go on showing until they are able to find somebody else.' Her mother was stern.

Charlie raised his eyebrows. He was going to say, 'They'll never find anyone as good as Shrimp,' but decided not to add to her already enlarged opinion of herself. Everyone was amazed that she was prepared to give up showing for the useless little scrap of a foal, which she christened Bonzo.

To give him his due, Bonzo had a strong inclination to live, in spite of his bad beginning. Although weedy, he had great determination, and scrabbled to his feet whenever anyone came near, eager for his bottle. Even Charlie admitted that he was a tough little character. Charlie even stooped to feeding him when Joan had to be away from home for more than two hours, although this happened rarely and nobody knew but Joan. Shrimp set up a camp-bed in the foal's loose-box with an alarm clock nearby, and the bottles made up ready and keeping warm in an old hay box, and she was the one who did the midnight to dawn watch, without any complaint. Rowan was allowed by her parents to do two nights a week up to eleven o'clock, when her mother came to fetch her in the car, but she rarely went to sleep. She was quite happy to lie there watching the foal, or staring out at the dusk and the first stars, thinking how lucky she was to have this second home at High Hawes. Even without her own pony, she was happy just to be accepted into the Hawes yard.

Babar made the appointment for them to ride at the Half Moon Riding Stables two Saturdays after Bonzo was born. Rowan was crossing the days off on her calendar, and thought she would be sick with excitement when the time came.

'Reckon he'll 'ave quieted down, working in a hire stable,' Babar commented. ''E might be just the job for you now.'

Rowan still had her dream of owning Swallow and riding with Lizzie and Hugh up across the downs on her own pony. And with Charlie too – for now that Fedora had no foal to look after, Charlie had taken to riding her out, just walking for an hour or two in the evening before it got dusk. Rowan's dream grew more star-studded . . . to riding with Charlie across the downs in the cool of the evening, the horses close together on the smooth turf . . . cantering in the moonlight, following the red whisk of Fedora's tail . . .

Fedora, rid of her encumbrance, was growing back into the elegant thoroughbred racehorse she was bred to be. With work, her neck and quarters filled out with muscle, and her dull demeanour was sloughed off. Her eyes were bright again, and her coat gleamed with good health. She looked about her with her ears pricked, her gaze alert.

'She was worth an old engine, eh?' Charlie said with satisfaction. 'It didn't go, anyway.'

The Saturday morning designated for the ride at the Half Moon Stables arrived at last. Although it was flaming June, the fields were shrouded in soft rain. But Rowan's excitement was not to be quenched, and she met Babar at the bus stop dressed in her new jods and the tweed jacket she had borrowed from Lizzie.

Babar looked just the same in her muddy anorak and green gumboots, swinging her grey skull-cap by its strap. Rowan had read in books that it was bad to ride in gumboots and hoped she wasn't going to feel ashamed of Babar. She was then ashamed of this thought. The bus came on time, in fact two minutes early, and as it moved off she could feel her legs literally trembling with excitement. She pressed her knees hard together. It was bound to be a disappointment, she told herself. Nothing could live up to such expectations as she had woven in her dreams. As if guessing her thoughts, Babar said, 'It might not be such a wow, this riding stable. It won't be like High Hawes, you know.'

The Half Moon Riding Stables proved to be a yard of jerry-built sheds with tin roofs situated at the far end of a small industrial estate. Rowan had to adjust her expectations immediately, walking down the drive between lorries and workshops sparking out purple sprays of acetylene torches. She felt sick again, and her face was white. Babar was thinking that this visit might be a mistake, but kept her thoughts to herself. Rowan, she knew, had the usual urban view of animal life, giving animals human emotions. But a pony didn't care if its stable was falling down as long as it was fed and had its companions around it and was treated sensibly. There were more unhappy ponies overfed and underworked, overheated in thermal rugs in cosy stables, than there ever were out in the fields apparently neglected. But it was too late to start propounding such theories to the dismayed Rowan.

Sadly, the tatty stables were a sign of Laura Griffiths's trouble with money. Laura Griffiths was knowledgeable and meant well, but was a hopeless organizer and had no business head. Her stables were falling apart in more ways than one.

The usual contingent of girls were milling around outside the yard, tacking up some scurfy ponies with straw in their tails. The ponies stood dejectedly, laying back their ears as their bridles were dragged on. The saddles, although clean, were old-fashioned and worn-out. Laura Griffiths came out of the tack room and saw them. Her habitual worried frown deepened.

'Oh, you're the girls from High Hawes who booked. One of you wanted to ride Swallow?'

'Yes,' said Babar.

'Well, you're going out with Fiona and Sharon, and you can swap ponies if Swallow is—' she hesitated. 'If he doesn't suit,' she decided on.

It was only then that Rowan realized that one of the scurfy ponies was Swallow. She hadn't recognized him. He was standing with his head down and his eyes half-shut, his bright coat staring dully and all the roundness and bounce disappeared. While she stood, her jaw dropping with dismay, the girl plonking a saddle with no stuffing onto his back said to her, 'It's you that wants him? I'm going to ride Fable and if he's naughty we can swap. Your friend can have The Armchair and Sharon'll take Snowball.'

'Good,' said Laura, and went back into the tack room. If she had noticed Babar's gumboots she wasn't going to say anything.

Rowan went up to Swallow and put her arms round his neck. He made no response, beyond sighing deeply. Fiona gave his girths a great heave, which provoked a cross grunt, and Swallow took a sharp nip at Rowan's arm. She jumped back, shocked. Babar said quickly, 'Lots of 'um snap when you pull up the girth.' Then she added, despite herself, 'Poor littl'un. 'E's lost his spirit.'

Was spirit something that could be

repaired? Rowan was now so disappointed she didn't even want to ride. But Fiona was holding Swallow and expecting her to mount. She hopped up and settled herself in the excruciatingly uncomfortable saddle. Fiona shortened her stirrup leathers. Swallow stood like a pudding, head down. Rowan didn't see how he could possibly be naughty without any spirit.

The Armchair, Babar's mount, was well named, for in spite of his dirty coat and gaunt flanks, he was a naturally round and cheerful but rather ugly chestnut cob. He had a wide blaze and four white stockings and a rather humorous expression. Babar, settling herself, said, 'Cor, I can see why 'e's called Armchair.' Recalling Diamond's sharp spine and narrow shoulders, Rowan imagined he felt as different from Diamond as sitting on an apple would be to sitting on a fence. Fable was a dull-looking light bay mare of about fourteen two, rather like a down-market Birdie, and Snowball was a small white pony with a mulish look in his eyes.

When they were all mounted Fiona said, 'All right, then,' and led the way out of a gate at the back of the yard. To Rowan's relief she saw that they were not going to promenade through the industrial estate, but down quite a pleasant lane towards some woods and fields. Swallow walked sourly with his head down, his nose resting on Fable's tail. When Rowan tried to pull him out to go alongside he put back his ears and resisted stubbornly, not moving out of his track. Babar manoeuvred herself alongside.

'This 'un isn't 'alf comfortable,' she said.

Rowan tried to tell herself that she had achieved her heart's desire, to ride Swallow, but somehow it was nothing like her dreams. Fiona and Sharon rode in front, chatting, and Swallow stuck stubbornly to Fable's tail. At one point Fiona turned round and said, 'Swallow loves Fable. He always does that.' Rowan thought, He wouldn't if Hugh was riding him, but no-one expected her to try and dissuade him from his riding-school habits. Fable, like Swallow and Snowball, walked stiffly and slowly, head down and uninterested, shuffling her ill-shod feet. Rowan sat thinking of Cascade and Birdie and Fedora, with their alert ears and bright eyes. She didn't know horses could be so different. She had never thought about it. She didn't know.

'What's wrong with them?' she whispered to Babar.

Babar shrugged. 'Tired,' she said. 'Not enough grub, too much work, I daresay. This one's not bad though.'

When the lane petered out into a leafy track through the woods the ponies all shuffled into a slow trot without being told. Swallow's head was almost on his knees and when Rowan tried to collect him, as taught by her High Hawes instructors, he pulled back at her inexperienced hands and gave a buck which shot her up onto his neck. Grabbing the copious mane, she pushed herself back into place. She did not try to collect him again but resigned herself to bumping along on the awful saddle.

At the far end of the woods a gate gave into open grass fields where a well-trodden track ran alongside the hay crop. The minute they were through the gate the ponies all started to canter. Rowan, unwarned, nearly lost her seat. She took a pull at Swallow but he stuck his head out and took no notice. He seemed to have forgotten his love for Fable for he quickly overtook her and went to the front, travelling fast. Rowan had a suspicion that she was being bolted with. She heard Babar shout, 'Sit back! Sit back!'

The track stretched away ahead of her into

unbroken distance. Rowan tried to sit back although all her instincts were to lean forward and hold onto the flying mane. She was very unhappy and getting frightened, and tried to take a pull on the reins. Surely a pony stopped if you pulled hard enough? But once Hugh had said to her, 'It's not done by pulling.' Unfortunately he hadn't bothered to explain what it was done by, and Rowan had no idea. She leaned back and pulled hard. All of a sudden Swallow's neck and ears vanished and she was no longer aboard, but hitting the hard and unyielding earth with an almighty thump. All the breath was knocked out of her and she lay watching the sky reeling over her head, filled with black spots that certainly weren't birds. She made no effort to get up – it was so awful, all her eager excitement crushed by this crowning unglory. Swallow . . . her darling Swallow! Nearly killing her . . .

'You still alive?' Babar loomed overhead, very anxious.

'Yes, I'm all right.'

'The little beggar! He gave a huge buck! No wonder you came off.'

Babar got off and helped her get to her feet. When she looked round, she saw that

Swallow hadn't vanished into the distance but had stopped to crop hungrily at the grass. Fiona had caught him and was jerking his head up crossly.

'He always does that,' she said.

'Why ever didn't you say so?' Babar said indignantly.

'I thought she could ride.'

'Some instructor you are!'

'You're not paying to be instructed. This is a hack. You said a hack.'

'Huh!'

'She'd better ride Fable. She won't do anything.'

''Asn't got enough strength,' Babar said. 'Just as well.'

Fiona glared at her. She held Fable and Rowan struggled into the saddle. Babar shortened the leathers for her.

'Don't worry. This 'un'll be OK.'

They all set off again at a walk. Rowan felt groggy, but trusted the gentle mare whose long neck and ears seemed to stretch out into the distance ahead of her. She felt quite different from Swallow, and her saddle was marginally more comfortable. Babar rode beside her in her new motherly role, and Fiona took Swallow to the front, presumably able to overcome his desire to follow Fable. He went with his ears laid back, a mulish look in his eye.

'Do you want to canter again?' Fiona asked presently, over her shoulder.

Rowan didn't, but said she did, to preserve face.

Fable obviously didn't want to, and the problem this time was to make her lurch into a canter from a longer and longer trot. Rowan rolled all round the saddle in her efforts and was relieved that Fiona and Sharon were in front and not watching. Swallow didn't buck this time, but went fast with his ears laid flat back. When Fable eventually consented to canter, her stride was long and very easy. Rowan was amazed, never having found Diamond's canter very comfortable. Beside her Babar was bowling along, grinning. She too was finding out Diamond's shortcomings by comparison. But the pleasure was shortlived as Fiona turned out of the big field into a road and they dropped back into the dispirited walk. Fable had to be niggled at all the time to keep up. By the time they got back to the stable Rowan was exhausted.

They paid their money and were obviously

not expected to untack and put the ponies away. Laura came out and noted that Rowan had changed ponies but made no remark beyond, 'All right then?' Meaning, 'Still all in one piece?' by the faint look of surprise on her face.

There seemed to be nowhere to turn the ponies out, as they were taken back into the low-roofed sheds. Babar asked if they had no field and Laura, looking more worried still, said no, she'd lost her bit of grass to a builder in the new year.

Before Rowan had a chance to take an emotional farewell of Swallow (and probably get bitten for her pains), Babar hurried her away, saying they had a bus to catch.

'There isn't one till one o'clock,' Rowan pointed out.

'No,' said Babar, 'but I could do with a cup of tea and a bun.' She had no desire to linger in the depressing stable. She wanted it to appear better than it was to comfort Rowan, but Rowan was not so ignorant that she could not see the truth for herself. High Hawes had set her standards.

'That's a terrible place!' she despaired, white-faced, as they went back through the industrial estate. 'Poor Swallow!'

'We should 'ave let well alone,' Babar muttered.

'How can I get him out of there?'

'Ask your dad to buy 'um.'

'He never will, when he once had him for nothing.' Rowan knew the way her father's mind worked.

'No, and Fred Hawes won't, for the same reason. Especially as 'e knows the ownership could be doubted – 'e was stolen, like.' She tried to present the best case she could. 'They're not cruel, after all. 'E's not really ill-treated.'

Rowan, who now had a splitting headache, hadn't the heart to argue. They went and got a snack in a cafe and sat glumly on the bus home. Babar was not a talker. The only thing she said, in surprise, was, 'That Armchair – 'e gave me a good ride, run down as 'e was. 'E could be real nice, that one.'

'He's very ugly.'

'Looks aren't everything.'

No. Swallow had the looks, but had been beastly. Fable, knock-kneed and hollow-necked, had been gentle and kind. Only tired. When Rowan went up to High Hawes in the late afternoon, Lizzie and Hugh were just coming

148

back from the downs. Rowan saw the ponies with fresh eyes, their gleaming well-being and rounded muscle, the spring in their step.

'How was it?' Lizzie called out.

Rowan shrugged. 'All right,' she said.

CHAPTER NINE

Afterwards Rowan told Lizzie how awful it was. But no-one could think of a way of rescuing Swallow apart from buying him, and even the £10 notes in the coffee jar did not amount to nearly enough.

'They all need rescuing really, not just Swallow.'

When Charlie heard, he said to Rowan, 'You have to get it into proportion. Lots and lots of humans have a far worse life than Swallow. You can't save the world. He's not suffering or in pain or starving.'

'Not quite,' said Lizzie.

Hugh added, 'Charlie's suffering.'

Charlie gave him a hating look and went off to ride Fedora.

'What did Hugh mean by that?' Rowan asked Lizzie when they were alone.

'Oh, he's having a bad time with Dad. They don't get on. Charlie has to do as he's told and he doesn't like it. He ought to go and work for someone else really, but Dad can't do without him. Dad's terribly bad-tempered these days, since he was ill.'

Rowan had noticed. She kept out of Mr Hawes's way. He didn't seem to mind her being around, because she did a lot of mucking out and sweeping and tack-cleaning to pay her way, but mostly, she gathered, he gave short shrift to hangers-on. His yard was a professional dealing yard with usually some dozen or so high-class horses for sale and he and Charlie and Josephine looked after them without outside help. Charlie was the 'nagsman' who rode them for prospective buyers – or Josephine if it was a lady's horse. The front yard, which gave on to the road, was the dealing yard, with the boxes smartly painted and everything in its place. Behind the big haybarn and feed shed which made the far side of this yard, was the family yard where Birdie and Cascade and Fedora lived, and the 'problem horses' which came to be re-schooled. This was not nearly so smart, and was where the children were supposed to stay in their place. The house lay to the side, up the hill and was accessible from both yards through the garden where Joan Hawes spent all of her little spare time. The garden was rather wild but very beautiful now in the full height of summer, rampant with heavily-scented roses and old-fashioned hollyhocks and delphiniums. It was protected on the far side, up the hill, by an oak copse and the huge old trees gave a lovely sense of security and history to the farm, which Rowan was very aware of. She thought High Hawes was the loveliest home she had ever come across. When she mentioned this in her own home, her father said, 'It's run-down but it could fetch half a million if it was put in order.' That was the only way his mind worked.

'Mum's a garden nut,' Lizzie said. 'She doesn't like horses.'

But Rowan was sensitive to the strains in the Hawes family and knew that times were hard and all sorts of mutinies were suppressed behind Josephine's silences and Charlie's dark gypsy eyes.

She tried to take Charlie's sensible remarks to heart and stop thinking about Swallow. It wasn't as if she had owned him ever, or ridden him before. They tried giving her a few more lessons on Cascade, but she was frightened of getting bucked off and Charlie told them to lay off. 'You don't want to put her off for life.' Instead, in the school, he let her ride Fedora, but it was only as a sort of treat. There was no future in it. As she glided round on the lovely mare at the end of a lunge line, she felt herself on the edge of paradise. It made it worse, the wonderful feeling, afterwards . . . she had nothing to ride, when she wanted it so.

Her mother said, 'Next year, perhaps, we'll be able to buy you a pony. But it's such a lot of work, darling, and you'll lose interest in a year or two, you know you will.'

Rowan knew nothing of the sort. It wasn't like piano lessons, or ballet, for goodness' sake, both of which she would happily forgo.

Trying not to be miserable when she had so much anyway, she walked up to High Hawes for her session with Bonzo. Her mother would call for her soon after half-past ten. When the others had gone to bed, she settled herself on the old couch against the wall of the box and pulled the sleeping bag up round her legs. Bonzo as usual came over and pushed and shoved at her, wanting his next bottle already but she cuffed him away, as instructed – he wasn't to be spoilt – 'Some hopes!' said Charlie – and settled down to make herself comfortable. Shrimp always set the alarm clock, but Rowan hardly ever went to sleep. She was quite happy to lie watching Bonzo, or the square of soft dusk out of the top door, thinking how mostly lucky she was (except not having her own pony).

But tonight, no sooner was she settled, than Fred Hawes came into the yard with Charlie and stopped outside Bonzo's box.

He said, 'If you let this woman try Fedora, she's ready to pay four thousand. The mare is exactly what she's looking for. She doesn't want a performer, just a good-looking thorough-bred with reasonable manners.'

Charlie said, 'I'm not selling Fedora.'

'You'll do as I tell you, my lad. That mare is in my stables, eating my grub, and using up too much of your blooming time. You're not eighteen yet. I've told you before – I'm the one who gives the orders round here.'

'Yes, I've heard the whole flaming lot before! But Fedora's mine. She's not yours to sell!'

'Everything in these yards is mine to sell, lad. I think you're getting ideas above your station. This woman, Mrs Elsworth, is coming on Tuesday afternoon, and Fedora is the one . . .'

They passed on towards the house and

Rowan heard no more. She lay wide-eyed, astonished by the angry words. Sell Fedora! How could he, after all Charlie had done? Cascade and Birdie too . . . he would sell those – Hugh and Lizzie had always said he would if the right money were offered. She guessed Hugh would mind terribly if he lost Cascade. But Fedora! Fedora was different. No wonder Hugh had said Charlie was suffering. Rowan's loyal soul ached for Charlie as she lay thinking what was running through his mind. Her sadness over Swallow was as nothing to how he would feel about losing Fedora.

Afterwards, she wondered if she had dozed off and imagined the conversation. When she got home she fell into bed and slept heavily, and found it difficult to get up when she was called in the morning. It was important to look bright and shiny at the breakfast table after her nights with Bonzo, in case her mother would stop her going. She was anxious to ask Lizzie if it was true that Fedora might be sold. But when she got to the school bus stop there was no sign of any of the children from High Hawes and, although the bus driver waited a few minutes extra, they didn't come. Rowan got on with Babar and they both tried to surmise what had stopped them coming.

'It's very odd, all of 'em,' Babar said. 'They can't all be ill.'

'Something must have happened.'

But what? Rowan was on pins all day, trying to connect their absence with the row between Fred Hawes and Charlie. But how could it have any consequence?

When she got home she rushed to change out of her school clothes to go up to High Hawes. But her mother said quietly, 'You can't go up there tonight. Fred Hawes has died.'

Rowan was stunned. 'But—' He was aggressively well only a few hours ago. 'He can't—!'

'He had another heart attack and died immediately. It's terribly sad. Joan Hawes is very calm – I rang her to see if there was anything we could do – but she seemed to be coping. She said she would let me know.'

Rowan burst into tears, shocked by the blow to the family. Whatever would they all do without Fred to run the stables and business? Their whole life revolved round the horses. Fred was the lynchpin. She could see her own life falling apart . . . the farm put up for sale, Charlie going away . . . the ponies . . . Bonzo . . . 'Oh no!' It was awful. For Fred Hawes she felt less compassion than for her friends, left abandoned. Her mother put her arm round her, not realizing the selfishness of her dismay.

'There, these things happen. It's very sad. Don't get upset. You can ask Lizzie and the others down here if Joan Hawes wants them out of the way – Lizzie can stay the night, perhaps, if it would help.'

Charlie needn't sell Fedora now! Rowan seized on the only ray of light and nursed it, remembering Charlie's agonized, 'Fedora's mine! She's not yours to sell!' He was saved.

The next day, Lizzie and Hugh were on the school bus. They were subdued, but otherwise showed no great signs of grief. Rowan somehow felt in awe of them. Death was a big subject. She didn't know what to say. But Lizzie wasn't inhibited.

'Charlie wants to go on running the business, but Mum's rather doubtful. She thinks it's too much – he's too young and all that stuff. But none of us wants to move. Dad's brother's coming today – he thinks he's going to tell us all what to do but we hate him. Uncle Trevor. That's why Hugh and me decided to come to school, to keep out of his way. And Mum wants us out of the way too. Shrimp won't stop crying, she couldn't come. She thinks she might lose Bonzo. I don't think it's Dad she's crying for.'

She looked out of the window and was silent for a little while. Rowan didn't know what to say. She kept trying to think what it would be like if her father died, and couldn't. More peaceful was all she could come up with. She had a feeling that her mother might even be relieved: she spent so much time worrying about not upsetting him. Where did love come into it? Rowan loved Charlie more than her father. Or did she? It was very hard to know what exactly love was. Fred Hawes had not been very lovable, in her opinion, but if he was your father it must be different. She couldn't very well ask Lizzie if she had loved him. In the end they didn't say anything much, but talked about the end-of-term play they were going to perform in.

*   *   *

Joan Hawes said sharply to Charlie, 'I don't care what your opinion of Uncle Trevor is. He's coming to help and you must be civil. As it is, I haven't ten pounds in my purse at the moment and there's no way of getting anything out of the bank, the way your father has left his affairs. Everything is in his name. It doesn't seem to occur to you that I might *need* help just at this moment.'

'I'll help you,' Charlie said.

'Oh yes? You borrowed five pounds off me on Saturday, remember?'

Charlie glared at her and slammed out of the room. When Uncle Trevor's black Rover slid into the drive beside the house he went out the back way and made for the stableyard. Uncle Trevor was a butcher with oily hair and a smarmy manner. They all hated him. Even their father had hated him. Charlie suspected he would try and buy High Hawes; he had tried once before when Fred had owed money, but had been sent packing by his derisive brother. Now he probably thought he had their mother at his mercy. She was not experienced in business affairs; her husband had kept the books and, although she knew they had little money to spare, she had been shocked by the situation outlined by the bank manager earlier in the day. Charlie could not bear to see his indomitable mother scared into accepting help from the reviled Uncle Trevor.

Josephine had driven off to see a dealer whom their father had been due to visit. She, without saying anything, had stepped into their father's shoes. Perhaps it was just to tell the man Fred Hawes had died. Charlie had no idea. Perhaps it was time he and Josephine should start talking. They had got on together all this time by instinct, knowing which of them did what, but always in the shadow of their father. Charlie felt as if he had been leaning against a stone wall, and the wall had fallen down. There was no ground underneath him. There was no past and no future.

A smart grey Audi drove into the front yard. He could see it through the window in the back of Fedora's box. A woman got out and looked round. She was middle-aged and well dressed in riding clothes. Someone for their father no doubt. Charlie went round to see what she wanted.

'Mr Hawes?' she said. 'I'm Mrs Elsworth. We spoke on the phone.' She held out her hand in a business-like way.

Charlie shook it. He could think of nothing to say.

'You said you had a mare that might suit me. I haven't found anything I like so far. Could I see her?'

She looked round at the few curious heads

which were looking out over the top-doors. They had turned out half the inmates, having had no time to ride them all out. 'A chestnut, he said.'

Charlie said, 'She's round here.'

He led the way to the home yard and opened Fedora's box.

'I'll lead her out for you.'

He had done it hundreds of times, trotted a horse out on the concrete, forward and back, saddled and bridled it, taken it into the manège. Mrs Elsworth watched him with keen, knowledgeable eyes. She held Fedora while he fetched his helmet. He mounted and rode Fedora into the school.

She had never gone better. Kind and willing, she circled, backed, did a half-pass in both directions, and jumped the bars in the centre. He rode as if in a dream, and Mrs Elsworth saw a perfect horse being ridden by a perfect rider. She had been looking for such an exhibition for six months and had thought, recently, it would never happen. She leaned on the gate, watching with her green hawk eyes. The boy had hands like silk, and the authority of his body communicated to the mare without any obvious signals. She was impressed by his quietness and his rather distant demeanour. His face was taut and pale and he did not smile.

When he came back to the gate he slipped off, and shortened the stirrup leathers to her length.

'You want to try her?'

'I will, but I hardly need to. She's exactly what I'm looking for.'

She rode well enough herself, but knew she would never achieve the boy's mastery. She was fifty, after all.

'I'll give you a cheque now.'

'For four thousand?'

'That's what I understood.'

'She might not pass the vet. She's got scars on her back legs, wire scars.'

'I don't want to show her. It doesn't matter.'

'Don't you want her vetted?'

'I'll give you a post-dated cheque, and get her vetted by my own vet at home. You'd agree to that?'

'Yes.'

'Very well. I'll call and collect her in the morning.'

She gave Charlie the cheque and drove away. He took it into the house and put it on the table in front of his mother. It was made out in her name.

'That's for you.'

She stared at him. Tears were trickling down his cheeks. Uncle Trevor looked at him spitefully.

'All this playing about with horses . . . you'll have to get out and find yourself a man's job, now your father's gone.'

Charlie gave him a look of utter contempt and went out, back to the yard, slamming the door behind him.

CHAPTER TEN

Rowan did not go to Fred Hawes's funeral but she helped at the reception afterwards in the house, when family and close friends went back for tea. Her mother was a very good cook, and offered to help Joan and, rather unexpectedly, Joan Hawes took her up on it. Joan was worn out with shock and worry, and Rowan's mother, seeing her condition, took on herself the whole business of the funeral reception, and did it very efficiently. Rowan helped her hand round cups of tea and offer cakes. There were a lot of people there, all the local farmers and horse people as well as a vast number of family. The farmhouse was packed, visitors spilling out into the garden. As at most funerals, they all seemed very jolly, considering the circumstances, many of them meeting long-forgotten friends and family after a period of years. Rowan thought it very odd, but her mother said most funerals turned out like that.

'It's a compliment to the dead person, in a way, if everyone enjoys themselves. It shows he had a lot of jolly friends. If only a few people turn up and are very mournful, it's no help to the widow and family, after all.'

Rowan hardly recognized Charlie in his dark suit and black tie with his hair combed down and his good manners on show. She had not spoken to him since before Fred died, and found it hard to believe that he had sold Fedora after all. She had told no-one of the conversation she had overheard. Her heart ached for him, as she noted his strained look and the obvious effort it was taking to make polite conversation to his relations. But she had little chance to indulge her mooning over him, for her mother soon had her in the kitchen washing up. Gradually all the visitors dispersed, until, at last, only the family was left. Uncle Trevor and his fat blonde wife were the last to leave, with promises to return in a few days 'to sort things out'.

When they had gone, Charlie picked up a glass of wine someone had left and held it up.

'Here's to Uncle Trevor dropping dead like Dad!'

'Charlie, really!' Joan looked shocked, and then, suddenly giggled. 'Hear, hear,' she said.

'Hear, hear!' shouted Hugh.

'Hear, hear!' shouted Lizzie.

Everyone sat down round the big kitchen table, exhausted from the strains of the day. Joan pulled a chair out for Rowan. 'You've been working like a Trojan – I can't thank you enough!'

Rowan was thrilled with a great sense of belonging, and the fact that her mother was sitting down at the table too gave her enormous pleasure. Up till now she had always had an uneasy feeling that her parents resented her passion for High Hawes, but now she believed her mother had fallen under their spell as well, as she looked flushed and happy as she poured out fresh tea. She had certainly done a splendid job.

Charlie and Josephine sat side by side at the top of the table, in Fred Hawes's old place. Josephine looked immaculate in a navy-blue silk dress, with her blonde hair pulled back from her face. She had very clear, pale skin and serene grey eyes, the same colouring as all the others, except gypsy Charlie.

Rowan saw her smile, and say something softly to Charlie. She saw suddenly a rapport between them that she had never noticed before. She saw Charlie smile as well, and a sort of glittering look came into his eyes.

'Mother,' he said.

They all looked at him.

'Josephine's got something for you.'

Josephine passed an envelope up the table to Joan.

'I sold two of the horses the day after Dad died, to Sid Palmer,' she said. 'And he gave me the money just now. Three thousand each. With the money from Fedora, that's ten thousand Charlie and I have made you this week. We think you can tell Uncle Trevor to take a running jump. We can run the business, if you'll let us.'

'Yes, yes!' shouted Hugh.

'Yes!' shouted Lizzie.

'Yes, you must!' screamed Shrimp.

Even Rowan found herself saying, 'Yes, *please*! Please do!'

Joan opened the envelope, looking dazed. 'It's in my name! I'm really rich – I've never had a penny of my own for years!'

'We've been discussing it, Josephine and I,'

Charlie said. 'Will you hear our plans, and let us try to make a go of it?'

'I don't want all this, you know,' Joan said. 'You must take it back, for the yard.'

'We've got six more horses to sell – of Dad's,' Charlie said, 'And the Prebbles want Birdie. With that money we thought we could set up a school, like you've always said we should. It was your idea, after all. Go more for children and children's ponies. We thought we could even take holiday weeks – kids staying here and riding out each day, and intensive week's courses. Cross-country courses, or day rides – whatever might make the money. And the Pony Club's always wanting somewhere for a course, and rallies. Dad would never have them. But we could. And we can still do Dad's dealing, with his connections, but not rely just on that, like he did. We can take duff ponies and Hugh and Shrimp can school them to sell – things like that. I'm sure we can make us all a living.'

'We don't want to go away,' Josephine said.

'No,' Charlie said. 'We belong here.'

'You *can't* go away, either of you!' Lizzie cried out. 'It would be awful here without you!'

Joan Hawes shook her head, looking rather weepy. 'I'm sure I don't want either of you to get other jobs. It's just that I don't want you to take on so much responsibility – keeping us all and the roof over our heads. You're so young for that! You want some fun in life.'

'Oh, come on, Mum, can't you see – the way Dad worked us – it won't be any different!'

'But you didn't have the worry of it. He did all that. It's probably what killed him.'

'Yes, but there's lots of us – Josephine and me now, and in no time Lizzie and Hugh and Shrimp. At least we can give it a try – surely?'

'It's very early days to take decisions. But I must say I can't stand the thought of Trevor taking us over. He's really set on interfering.'

'You know it's the farm he wants,' Josephine said. 'Helping us – so-called – is just his way of getting his nose in. Dad always steered clear of him, didn't he? Dad wouldn't want it. He would want us to carry on, I'm sure.'

'Well, your father did build this place from nothing. It was all in ruins when we came here. He was proud of what he'd done.'

'Sleep on it, Mum,' Charlie said. 'You haven't got to decide now this minute. But you've got some money now, and time to think, and you can tell Uncle Trevor to get stuffed when he turns up.'

'I must say, I would like that.'

'Well, for the time being—' Charlie glanced at Josephine again, and Rowan noticed that the strained look had gone from his face and he looked like his old self. He pushed his chair back from the table. 'I'm going to change. There's work to be done.' He laughed.

Josephine got up too. 'Yes. I hate dresses.'

'So do I!' shrieked Shrimp, jumping up. 'I've got to feed Bonzo!'

Joan turned to Mrs Watkins and said, 'One thing about animals, they always need looking after, whatever happens. You can't take to your bed when there's a stableful of horses outside.'

'Yes. Quite a responsibility.'

Mrs Watkins thought it was time to go. She had only stayed so long because Joan had pressed her to. Rowan was amazed at how her mother had got on with Mrs Hawes, and how they had been accepted as part of the family.

Later, Lizzie said to her, 'It's funny, but it's much nicer at home now Dad has gone.'

Rowan was horrified by this remark.

Lizzie said, 'He only ever shouted at us. And he and Charlie didn't get on at all. There was always a nasty sort of feeling around, Dad getting at Charlie, and Josephine not saying anything, sort of stuck between them. Now it's all right. More sort of relaxed. And Josephine's started to talk more.'

Rowan was amazed. She told her mother this, and her mother wasn't amazed at all, but just said, 'Well, I understand he was a difficult man. And those older two – young people need their freedom, to work out their own lives. It's not a very good idea for a boy to work for his father, without seeing something of the world first. It makes sense to me, that Charlie's much happier now he's his own boss.'

It seemed that Uncle Trevor had been sent packing. Lizzie and Hugh giggled about it, describing how he went red with rage, and stalked out, and backed his car into the water-trough and dented the wing.

'All the same,' Mrs Watkins said, 'they've got a lot on their plates. They're only children.'

Rowan didn't think of Josephine and Charlie as children, but supposed she saw it from a different point of view.

In spite of what Lizzie said, she and the others were more subdued after the funeral, and Rowan saw Hugh crying in Cascade's box, when he thought no-one was there. Shrimp kept bursting into tears too, and Lizzie would get into a temper about nothing at all, which she never did before. Joan Hawes looked terrible. Perhaps Fred Hawes hadn't been the easiest man in the world to live with, but it was apparent that they all missed him dreadfully. He had been the rock on which their lives had rested. Perhaps, when rocks moved, the shock took some time to sink in. Certainly the atmosphere at High Hawes had changed, and the time of grieving was something the family had to bear. Nobody talked about it, but Rowan sensed the tension, and took care to tread carefully.

It was nearly school holidays and, since the plans for a riding school had been aired, the children rather thought that High Hawes would be flooded with new ponies overnight, but nothing seemed to happen, save that Charlie bought a pony very cheap because it had a bad knee. It couldn't be ridden for the time being. It was a Welsh mountain, small and strawberry roan and very pretty, but Rowan thought it was too small for her, even when it was better. Shrimp christened it Pinkie. It was turned out in the field.

Birdie was advertised for sale. On the evening

of the day the ad appeared in 'Horse and Hound' Mrs Prebble appeared in the yard with Matty.

It was hot and they were out in the field watching Bonzo learning to eat grass. Shrimp had him on a halter, finding him luscious tufts, because the novelty of staying up all night to feed him was fast wearing off. Charlie was in the manège exercising one of the yard horses which had been advertised at the same time, and Josephine was doing feeds in the feed shed.

Birdie was in, because of the ad, and Lizzie had been grooming her diligently, so that her light bay coat gleamed and her black points shone like satin, and her black mane lay neatly on one side. Charlie had promised Lizzie she could have a 'nice' pony when Birdie was sold. 'Like Babar's Diamond,' he said, laughing. 'Cheap. It will have to be cheap.' He went out looking for bargains, but they were few and far between. There was always something wrong with them. Pinkie was the only one he had come back with so far.

When Mrs Prebble came into the yard they all came to attention.

Hugh gave Lizzie a great nudge and said, 'Go on. Tell her she's five thousand pounds.

She pays whacking prices for Matty's ponies.'

Lizzie got up nervously. 'Will I have to ride her? With that Matty watching?'

'Yeah. Of course. Don't be such a booby.'

'Can't you?'

'She's your pony.'

While they argued, Charlie rode out of the school and dismounted to talk to Mrs Prebble. Rowan, seeing she was needed, went up and took his horse for him. Matty stared at her in her usual haughty way. She was about fourteen, slender but with a very tough look about her, her eyes hard and supercilious. She was dark, and had pink cheeks and very white teeth, and a natural scowl. Rowan hated her on sight.

'I saw your ad,' Mrs Prebble said to Charlie. 'I don't know why you didn't give me a ring first. I told your father I was interested in that pony.'

Rowan had heard Charlie say he would put the cost of the ad on to the price if Mrs Prebble bought Birdie. He hadn't wanted to make any sort of an appeal to this famously aggressive and unpleasant woman. Hugh called her Hitler. She hadn't got a black moustache, but she had black shiny hair hanging over her fore-head to one side like Hitler, and wore leather boots, even on a summer evening. Rowan felt really grateful that she didn't have her for a mother, like poor Matty. Perhaps Matty scowled because she had Hitler for a mother.

Josephine came and took the horse off Rowan, but then disappeared, leaving the selling bit to Charlie. Charlie brought Birdie out of her box, and called for Lizzie to come and tack her up. Mrs Prebble examined her closely all over, as if looking for nits, and lifted up all her legs and pulled them about, and peered into the pony's mouth.

'She's five,' Charlie said.

'I'm not blind,' said Mrs Prebble.

'Only horrible,' whispered Hugh.

Lizzie was looking pale and was obviously deciding that, now the moment had come, she loved Birdie and didn't want to sell her. Charlie made her ride her in the school to show her paces, but was kind enough not to make her jump. He knew she hated riding in front of the Prebbles. But Matty wanted to jump her herself, and Charlie went off to put up the bars. Mrs Prebble leaned on the gate, frowning. Lizzie and Hugh and Rowan sat on the fence watching.

Matty was a forceful and effective rider, with none of Lizzie's misgivings, and Birdie looked surprised and rather nervous. Rowan felt sorry for her. When faced at the jump, she had no chance at all to refuse or run out, ridden with such skill and precision. Fred Hawes had always declared she had a jump like a kangaroo, and Rowan now saw how she had won this reputation, as Matty insisted that the jump was raised. Charlie looked slightly anxious, but was aware that he had a job of selling to do. To show doubt would be fatal. He put the jump up to three foot ten, and Birdie cleared it easily, then four foot. Again, so firmly was she presented, she flew over it.

'That's enough,' he said.

'Can we have her on trial?' Mrs Prebble asked.

'No. We don't let horses go on trial.'

'Not even half a mile away? You know us.'

'No.'

'You're being ridiculous.'

Charlie flushed up. How rude the woman was! They all sat agog, intrigued. But Matty slipped off and Charlie turned to undo Birdie's girths as if the selling was finished. Lizzie went to help him.

'She felt great, Mum,' Matty said, looking eager.

Mrs Prebble glared at her.

'That's as may be. How much are you asking?' she demanded of Charlie.

'Two thousand five hundred and fifty,' Charlie said.

'I'll give you two thousand, if she passes the vet.'

'No offers. The price is two thousand five hundred and fifty.'

'That's ridiculous. She's done nothing.'

'No, but she can.'

'It's a pity I'm not dealing with your father.'

Charlie turned away, to stop himself from saying something he might regret, and indicated that he had other things to do than stay talking to Mrs Prebble. Mrs Prebble turned on her heel and strode out of the yard. Lizzie and Hugh and Rowan all went into Birdie's box to give vent to their feelings. Lizzie burst into tears and said, 'I'm not selling dear Birdie to those beastly people!'

But on the school bus the next morning she said Mrs Prebble rang up at ten o'clock and agreed to Charlie's price, with a vet's certificate. Charlie told Lizzie he would buy some nice ponies with the money and she could have the one she liked best.

A dreamy look came into her eyes. 'A darling sweet pony who does exactly what I want, and never tanks off, or shies at things in the hedge.'

'You are *feeble*,' Hugh said in tones of great scorn. 'It's not as if you can't ride. And anyway,' he added, 'I think Charlie and Josephine ought to get horses for themselves, now we've got all this money – before you, because you're always saying you don't like it. And they do.'

'I would on a nice pony!'

'It's not fair on them not having anything.'

'They've still got six in the yard.'

'None of them are what they want, for their own. They're all heavyweight hunters, or stupid. And Charlie – giving his Fedora money all to Mum—' Words failed him.

'That was noble,' Shrimp said solemnly.

'I'll say! He made a whacking profit, though. I suppose he couldn't resist it.'

Rowan said nothing. She knew Charlie could have resisted it very well. Fedora was the horse he wanted. Perhaps he didn't want another one. It was true that he was noble.

'Well, he won't have time to ride his own

now, if he's got to give riding lessons to little girls. I can't see him, somehow . . .' Hugh looked doubtful. 'It's pretty yukky, after all, giving riding lessons to little girls.'

'You're a sexist pig,' Lizzie said. 'Little boys fall off and cry, and girls always get on again. That's why there's so few boys in the Pony Club, because they're always falling off and crying, and they won't come again. All the instructors say that.'

'I didn't cry! I got on again!'

'Oh, that's because you're so exceptionally marvellous and talented. Ugh!' Lizzie shuddered.

'Yes,' said Hugh.

Now Lizzie had nothing to ride she was very cross.

'No pleasing some people,' Charlie grinned.

Babar brought Diamond up again, for Rowan, but only two could ride out together, on Diamond and Cascade.

'Where are all these ponies you were going to buy?' they clamoured at Charlie.

'I'm working on it,' he said.

It was true that he went out a lot, and read all the ads in 'Horse and Hound' with great attention, but the feeling was that he was looking for a cheap youngster for himself, and one for Josephine. They bought an unbroken three-year-old for the dealing yard, which they thought was cheap at the price (but not good enough for themselves) and they sold one of the heavyweight hunters and one of the Irish job lots that Fred had imported.

'We're not exactly doing nothing,' Charlie countered their complaints.

Two weeks before the end of term both Charlie and Josephine went out with the big lorry. It hadn't been driven since Fred died – they always used the Land-Rover and trailer – and Hugh and Lizzie decided they had found two big youngsters for themselves. Or even one. Unbroken youngsters usually loaded more easily into a lorry than a trailer. They were both very mysterious about their trip and refused to take Hugh and Lizzie with them, although there was room in the cab.

'As if we want an outing in the old crate,' Hugh said sniffily.

Crossly, he went off for a ride with Babar. Lizzie and Shrimp and Rowan took Bonzo for a walk through the woods and out onto one of the downs tracks, and they lay in the grass while Bonzo practised his grazing, and Lizzie moaned about having no pony to take to Pony Club camp.

'I've never not been to Pony Club camp,' she said.

'I thought you didn't like it,' Shrimp said.

'I do now I can't go,' Lizzie said.

Rowan lay in the grass feeling its warmth underneath her and watching the little blue butterflies hovering over the flowers whose names she (being a town girl) didn't know. She couldn't imagine being back in Putney again, and yet this time last year . . . extraordinary! The sky was palest nothing-colour, the sun still high over the cockscomb of trees that crowned the nearest down. Near at hand Bonzo's new teeth and eager gums did their best on the fine turf and his bright eyes watched warily in the wide open spaces that were new to him. He hated being out in the field without a human nearby, and followed Shrimp everywhere like a dog around the yards and garden, even into the kitchen, until Joan had got cross. 'In bed next – I'm putting my foot down!' Rowan loved Bonzo and was pleased when he accorded her almost the same status as Shrimp. When he could eat grass he was going to be turned out in a small field with Pinkie, to see if Pinkie might be motherly towards him.

'Not like beastly Fedora.'

'She wasn't beastly,' Rowan said loyally. 'Motherhood didn't suit her. She was gentle otherwise. She couldn't help feeling like that.'

They got up and slowly went back down the hill, Bonzo following. From the chalk track above they could hear Babar and Hugh coming back, their voices carrying on the still evening air. They went through the oak wood and down the ride that led into the fields by the manège. Bonzo cantered on ahead, bucking, but had to wait by the gate. Shrimp haltered him to lead him through the field where other horses were grazing.

'I can hear the lorry,' she said.

They were all curious as to what Charlie and Josephine were bringing back. Hugh and Babar came trotting into the yard at the same moment as Charlie pulled up in the home yard. When he cut the engine, there was a lot of kicking from inside in the lorry and, suddenly, a whinny that stopped Rowan in her tracks.

She looked up, as Charlie jumped down

from the cab. He was grinning. He caught her eye and winked.

'Cheer up, Rowan, it's your lucky day.'

'You've bought *hundreds*!' Shrimp shouted.

They all crowded round as Charlie and Josephine let down the ramp and opened the doors.

'A job lot,' Charlie said. 'One each and some to spare. We've got the foundation of the High Hawes Equestrian Centre here.'

He skipped up the ramp. 'Here's yours, Shrimp!'

First down the ramp was the small white pony, Snowball. Rowan recognized him immediately. Also the next to follow:

'Lizzie, one for you. Name of Fable.'

The kind, thin, bay mare which Rowan had ridden stumbled down the ramp and Lizzie stepped forward dubiously to take her halter.

Next came the big white blaze of the washy chestnut cob which Babar had ridden. Babar came forward happily. 'Why, it's my old Armchair! I liked him!'

And last – 'Rowan!'

Rowan could hardly move for trembling knees nor see for helpless tears as Swallow came barging down the ramp.

'Manners! Manners!' Charlie brought him up short with a sharp check on his head-collar. He laughed at Rowan's expression.

'Your pony, madam. A High Hawes hireling.'

Swallow stood still, seeing that he had arrived safely with all his friends and an apple was being proffered on the hand in front of him. He took it delicately, and shoved affectionately at Rowan's arm.

'Oh Swallow!' Rowan flung her arms round his neck.

'Where's mine?' shouted Hugh crossly.

'You've already got one. Cascade. And all these are yard horses. We aren't giving them to you for your own, only to look after. Muck out and feed and exercise. This is a joint exercise, remember – High Hawes Equestrian Centre.'

'Well, they are a skinny-looking lot,' Hugh said disgustedly. 'They look half-starved to me. I wouldn't want any of 'em.'

'No, well, it's nothing a good field of grass won't cure. And why do you think we got them cheap? The owner couldn't afford to keep them.'

'There's another one still in the box,' Lizzie said. 'Whose is that?'

'That's mine,' Charlie said quietly.

He went up the ramp again to the horse hidden at the back of the big lorry. Josephine was smiling.

'He's gone mad,' she said to Lizzie. 'Look at it!'

They all laughed at the scarecrow that stumbled down the ramp, a very large, very thin bay gelding with an old-fashioned Roman nose and thick, puffy legs. He looked all round, blinking, as if to see what worse fate was in store, having come so low. He had dull, patient eyes, a ragged, rubbed mane, and a small white star on his forehead. Fedora had been poor, but compared to this one, she had been a queen.

Hugh stared. 'I don't believe it! Whatever would Dad say?'

Charlie looked, for him, quite sheepish.

'It's only five,' he said. 'It deserves a chance.'

'It's another for the knacker, like Fedora.'

'Exactly,' said Charlie. 'And look what I got for her!'

Hugh was squashed.

Charlie said, 'He'll be a nice horse one day. We've plenty of time. They've all had a raw deal and there's nothing that good food won't put right. For now they can all go out in the bottom field. They haven't seen grass for years, most of 'em.'

They led them out in a row, down the lane to the gate that let into an empty field. The field had been cut for hay, but already had a good new growth. Laura Griffiths's ponies couldn't believe their luck. One by one as they were led in and let loose they put their heads down and started wrenching at the grass. They didn't even stop to explore.

'Poor things!' said Shrimp. 'They're rescue horses!'

'No,' said Josephine, 'They're our new riding school ponies. We thought you could all go to the Pony Club camp after all.'

Was she teasing? Lizzie looked at her curiously in the dusk.

'On them?'

'There's a month to go. Why not? We'll get them wormed and well fed, and groom them, and you won't know them by August.'

'It's not very long.'

Charlie said, quite sternly, 'We haven't bought them for a lark. They've got to earn their keep, and the sooner the better. We need you all to go to Pony Club, to show everyone we're in business. It will get our name put around. We aren't going to make any money if we don't put ourselves out and about.'

'Us?' said Hugh. 'What about you?'

'Yes, we've already volunteered to help at camp. Josephine and I are going to do horse lines, and teach a bit. They've always wanted us – it was Dad who said we were too busy.'

'You always said it was a drag! You didn't mind not going!'

Charlie laughed. 'That's when I was always being told what to do. Now I'm going to do the telling. Nothing wrong with that.'

'You won't be teaching us!' Hugh looked alarmed. And then he added, 'At least I've got a decent pony, thank goodness.'

'Matty Prebble will take Birdie to camp, I bet,' Lizzie said, worried. 'Fable won't be the same—'

'Fable will look after you. You hated Birdie, remember?'

'I can take Snowball,' Shrimp said, 'I wouldn't mind that.'

'Thank goodness someone's pleased!'

Shrimp never went to camp ordinarily, as she had been too busy at shows. Her showing programme had dropped off since Bonzo, although she was still in demand.

And me? Rowan thought, but didn't say.

As they wandered back up the hill to home and supper, she felt isolated – scared and gloriously happy all at once. Was she really to take Swallow to Pony Club camp? It all seemed to be taken for granted. Could she cope – that was another question? Yet it was because of her badgering on about Swallow that they had discovered about Laura Griffiths and Charlie had bought his lorryload of 'bargains'. Inadvertently she had taken quite a hand in the fortunes of the new High Hawes Equestrian Establishment.

She had what she wanted. Hadn't she?

She walked back home, beside Babar riding Diamond. Babar too was quiet, and said, 'I really liked riding that Armchair. D'you think Charlie meant I could take 'um to camp, instead of Diamond?'

'I don't know.'

Rowan could see that Babar was torn, loyal to Diamond whom she had outgrown, not in size, but in satisfaction.

At the gate of the old hayfield they both stopped and looked down the valley at the new horses grazing. They were spread out now, their shadows long in the golden evening. They looked magical, the dusk cloaking their scurfy hides and poor sticking-out ribs.

'I reckon they think they're in paradise.' Babar smiled.

And me, Rowan thought. It had all come true for her.

And she suddenly felt free of all her doubts and misgivings, thinking of the courage with which Matty Prebble rode, and how noble Charlie had been over Fedora, and how devotedly little Shrimp cared for Bonzo, and how Joan Hawes had not buckled over with the death of her husband . . . she was amongst people who did not whinge, and to be one of them she must not be feeble and apprehensive.

She walked on down the hill beside Diamond. Her head was spinning. And Babar rode in thoughtful silence.

THE END

ABOUT THE AUTHOR

'There are very few born story-tellers. K.M. Peyton is one of them.'
THE TIMES

Kathleen Peyton's first book was published while she was still at school and since then she has written over thirty novels. She is probably best known for *Flambards* which, with its sequels *The Edge of the Cloud* and *Flambards in Summer*, was made into a 13-part serial by Yorkshire Television in 1979. *The Edge of the Cloud* won the Library Association's Carnegie Medal in 1969 and the *Flambards* trilogy won the *Guardian* Award in 1970. More recently, BBC TV televised her best-selling title *Who Sir? Me Sir?*

Kathleen Peyton is the author of a number of titles published by Transworld: *The Wild Boy and Queen Moon, The Boy Who Wasn't There, Poor Badger* (for younger readers) *Windy Webley* (for beginner readers) and, the following two titles in the High Horse series, *The Swallow Summer* and *Swallow, the Star*. She lives in Essex.

Now read the second title in the exciting *High Horse* series, THE SWALLOW SUMMER

Summer has come to High Hawes, and Rowan is still wondering if she'll *ever* be good enough to ride Swallow. However hard she tries to control him, her reckless pony seems to have a will of his own.

As if that isn't enough to worry about, Rowan's first Pony Club camp is looming, and Rowan is terrified it will be a disaster – she's bound to look a totally useless rider next to the brilliant Hawes family. But once at camp Rowan's worries are put into perspective when the future of the Hawes' riding school – including Swallow – is threatened. What really matters now is whether her darling horse can be saved – or is it to be sold . . .

0 552 529699

Don't miss the third title in K.M. Peyton's gripping High Horse series, SWALLOW, THE STAR . . .

Swallow looked boldly at the film people and the wind
blew his heavy mane up over his crest – Swallow the Star . . .

When a film company asks for a 'difficult' pony to appear in their new film, Swallow – Rowan's beautiful but very high-spirited pony – is everyone's first choice. But it is Rowan's talented friend, Hugh, who is picked to ride Swallow – not Rowan. And as Rowan watches Swallow put on a splendid performance for the cameras – throwing one enormous buck after another – she begins to have terrible doubts. Can she *ever* ride well enough to control her bold young pony?

0 552 529702